FEVER DREAM

By Barrett Newsom

First Paperback Edition

Published by BHNewsom Press, La Mesa, CA
bartnewsom@yahoo.com

Copyright 1998 by Barrett Newsom

ISBN 978-0-9847104-4-7

First Paperback Edition

Published by BHNewsom Press, La Mesa, California

Prologue

The Dream

The barricade came down at the railroad crossing ahead of him. Barry Sumner looked at his wristwatch but couldn't make out the time. It was either night or there was a storm brewing. The sky was an inky black in places and gray in others. Even the striped cross arm looked gray, the flashing lights along its length dim and without color.

The air smelled thick with moisture, like a garden hose in summer, hot and sticky to breathe. He realized he was almost out of breath, as if he had been running.

A signal bell clanged and Barry looked up at the crossed boards of the railroad sign, a reflector swinging back and forth under it. Then he heard the train.

Mournful, painful, like the cry of a great beast in agony, it came from his right. He looked down the tracks, two dull gray steel bands, somehow cold and hot at the same time. The train appeared as a dark apparition, without a headlight, approaching with rushing speed, terrible in its momentum. Behind the engine, a row of box cars trailed away, urging the train forward, as if the force of life itself pushed the massive locomotive closer and closer.

Barry suddenly knew the train was about to derail. He could feel the impending crash in his bones, as if every cell in his body had given out a loud shout, a shout he heard clearly above the roar of the train.

What could he do? He felt certain something he had done, something just out of reach of memory, was the cause. As if he had put a coin on the track, maybe just a penny, for the iron wheels to flatten into a paper-thin oval, shiny copper warm to the touch.

A vision of the train wreck flashed through him, huge pieces of metal flying every direction, a sound like a volcano erupting all around him. Just as quickly, he saw the train still approaching, as if in slow motion. Then the flash of the wreck again. Again the warm sensation of the smashed penny in his hand, the dread of guilt pressing on him like a great weight, making his heart ring like a steel spike driven by a sledge hammer. His ears pounded with the sound of the locomotive. Again he saw the cross arm, the flashing lights, heard the signal bell.

He cried out, his voice merging with the chaos around him.

Chapter 1

He awoke in a drenching sweat, his wife's hand on his breast. He could feel her cool fingers above his heart, which pounded hard in his ribs, heavy and rubbing against the walls of his chest like a water balloon tied to the spokes of a wheel. Pain wracked him and he realized his legs were cramping up.

He stifled his cries, looked at Martha's face in the dark, her eyes dark and deep with concern, beautiful and compassionate.

"Wake up, Barry. You're having a dream," she said.

He gulped a lungful of air, expelled it slowly through clenched teeth. *What a burden I'm becoming*, he thought - *worthless. They may as well take me out and shoot me.* Their room was silent, the sheets soaked with his perspiration. He sat up.

"I'm sorry I woke you up. I really had a whopper that time," Barry said. Uncontrollable shivers raced through him, his legs cramping again, and he rolled back on the bed with a groan.

"What is it?" Martha asked urgently. "What can I do for you?" She knelt on the mattress, helpless at his side.

"Cramps, cramps," he cried. "It's my legs. See if you can push my feet up. Oh, there it goes again." His calf muscles bunched up like two small cannon balls and he writhed on the sheets. *Christ,* he thought, half laughing to himself even in the midst of the pain- *I really am falling apart!*

A moment later, at the foot of the bed, Martha placed one of his feet on each of her shoulders and pushed like a linebacker on a tackling dummy. She was big, almost six feet, a good three inches taller than Barry, and equally strong. She really put her back into it and Barry pushed with all his might. The pain slowly subsided.

"Yes, yes, yes," he sighed as his muscles began to relax. "Yes, that's it. That's better now."

She turned on the reading lamp on her side of the bed before she sat down beside him again. In the light, he could see her breasts, full and free, silhouetted through the thin fabric of her nightgown. Gratefully, he extended his hand to her and brushed her nipples with his finger tips. She stiffened.

"Don't!" she said with finality. "Don't even think about it. I'm not in the mood and you're in no shape for sex."

Barry recoiled to his side of the mattress, punched a pillow. *Jesus,* he thought- *there's that rejection again. I really am pathetic. How could I be so stupid?* "I just wanted to thank you for helping me with my cramps," he said.

"Well, you can thank me by letting me get back to sleep. I have an important meeting tomorrow and I need rest." She snapped off the light, pulled the sheet up to her chin.

Like that, Martha reminded him of his mother after her gall bladder operation. She had lain in bed for weeks before getting up and about. Twelve years old, he'd kept her company that summer playing card games and dominoes. She had often held the sheet to her chin like that, joking with him about being in bed together. Her body was still slender and shapely, but she no longer looked young and pretty, the operation having added years to her face. Since that time, they had not been close, not nearly as close as when he was younger and she used to cuddle and caress him, stroke his hair using her fingers as a comb.

Memories flooded him as he stared up towards the ceiling and his heart thumped as he recalled the locomotive, the rush of speed.

"Wow," he said into the dark. "That really was a scary dream." He could feel blood pounding in his ears, which were hot and flushed.

A few seconds later, Martha answered, her voice calm and soothing, the remains of her Southern accent putting a soft edge on the night. "I really have to get some sleep. But if you want to talk, I'm here." He loved her voice, especially when she wasn't angry at him.

"It's just I've had that dream before, when I was a kid," he said. "I called it my fever dream."

"Why 'fever dream'?" Martha rolled onto her side, becoming the shadow of a mountain range on Barry's horizon.

"It's a dream I had whenever I got a high fever. I seemed to have a lot of them when I was young," he said. "When I got older, they gradually went away. I haven't had that dream in twenty years." A moment of silence passed before he added, "And never as vivid."

"It's just the Prozac, Barry," she pointed out matter-of-factly. "You're having lots of dreams lately."

"Whoa," Barry stopped her. "This wasn't just any old dream. This dream means something." He had no clue what, but was certain it was something dreadful.

"You want to tell me about it? All I can do is listen. I don't know shit about psychology."

"You don't even remember your own dreams, do you?" he asked skeptically.

"How should I know? I don't remember 'em," she quipped.

"This train is speeding towards me and I know it's going to crash. There's something terrible I did that is going to cause this crash, and the whole thing, the whole world is going to come apart."

"Wow," she said. "You don't mess around, do you? How about some lady smoking a cigar, something simple."

"I wish," Barry said. He could hear Martha thinking in the dark. Then she cleared her throat.

"Well, since you have the time off from work and I can't get you to do anything around the house, why don't you go down to the church and have a talk with Reverend Hanna about your dream. She gave a seminar down there last year on dream interpretation."

"I don't remember that," Barry said. "What was in the seminar?"

"How should I know?" Martha asked. "You won't catch me at one of those things. But Hanna's into it."

Barry had heard the lady priest at their church was into some far out stuff. There were rumors that her unorthodox habits continued into her bed, since she wasn't married and had no children of her own. That seemed natural to Barry, since she was a priest, after all, even if the Episcopal Church allowed its clergy to marry. It occurred to him that she might be a lesbian, but he didn't think it was any of *his* business. They'd had another priest who had been openly gay, or so the scuttlebutt said. Barry attended services a few times a year, the obligatory Christmas and Easter, since he'd been raised in the church and his parents still bugged him about it, but it didn't matter too much to him who the priest was. As long as the sermon was not too long and they didn't ask him for money every week.

Barry said that talking to Hanna sounded like a great idea. He'd give her a call in the morning and see if she had any appointments available. Meanwhile, he actually felt like a load had been lifted off his head, at least for the moment. He rolled over and gave Martha a kiss on the side of her face, nothing to get her riled up, thanked her again for helping him with his cramps, then settled into the still-damp sheets to go back to sleep.

As he snuggled his pillow, something happened that he hadn't felt for weeks - he began to get an erection. A warm wave of sexual feeling swept through him, but he didn't dare stir. No point in having another confrontation, he told himself. In his mind's eye, he saw faces and bodies from some of the women he knew at the office and he remembered his wife's silouette against the reading light, the touch of his fingers on her nipples. Had it been that long since they'd had sex? Then he heard soft snores coming from the other side of the bed.

Frustrated, he slid out of the covers, careful not to wake Martha, and padded to the bathroom barefoot. He left the light off. Again not wanting to wake her, he sat down to pee, his still-turgid member making it difficult. He didn't flush, but closed the lid quietly. At the sink, he waited for the water to get hot and his hard-on subsided. In the shadows, he saw himself in the mirror, his short-cut, salt and pepper hair all awry from the pillow, and the new goatee he'd begun. His whiskers were still a mix of red, brown and black, as though his gray was pre-mature. He knew, at 44, that nothing was pre-mature anymore. He washed his hands with soap, rinsed, then, before tuning off the tap, he drank deep, using his palms to cup the water, lapping it up like a dog.

Returning to bed, he watched the shadow of his wife sleeping deeply. Her breath was gentle now, barely rustling a lock of her chestnut hair that fell across her cheek.

How can she be so good for me and so bad for me at the same time? he wondered. *We probably won't have sex ever again.*

His mind refused to quiet as he stared into the darkness. Images of the dream returned, defying him to sleep. Just one small thing, one mistake, and his world would come flying apart. He closed his eyes but never got more than half asleep the rest of the night.

Down the hall from his parents' bedroom, Peter Sumner tried to go back to sleep. He'd been awakened by something strange, a noise he couldn't place, and now he lay in the dark listening to the sounds from his parents' room. There was grunting and heavy breathing, and he wondered half shocked if they were having sex.

He often wondered about that. They didn't even kiss good-bye in the morning before Mom left for work. Dad tried to talk to him about sex a few times, but Peter knew more than enough about it from those classes at school where teachers explained everything. Enough to know he didn't want anything to do with it. He was embarrassed enough about his body, what with being overweight and short and having big, fat feet, without wanting to take all his clothes off in front of some girl. However, he didn't think he'd mind if a girl wanted to take off her clothes in front of him. That might be a real laugh.

Whatever his parents were doing didn't last too long, and then he heard their voices, faintly in the night. Now they were having a conversation, although he couldn't hear what they were saying. He got out of bed and tip-toed over to his door, opened it a crack. Now he could hear their voices better, but still not well enough to make out the words. He stepped into the hallway, crept toward their door. In the dark, he could see shadows of pictures, dark squares on the darker wall. He kept absolutely quiet, not wanting to be discovered spying.

He figured they were talking about him, had to be. There had been a lot of fighting since Dad stopped going to work. In fact, before he'd quit, there had been one long argument every night for months. Peter just wanted things to get back to normal around the house. He wanted a normal summer so he and his dad could go back to the Sierras where they fished the year before. Peter hadn't been very good with a spinning rod, always needing help with some tangle or other, but it had been great to spend time, just Dad and him. He'd written a poem for English about it and got an A plus. *At Crystal Lake next to rugged mountains/ Rainbow trout leaped into fountains.* His dad had caught most of the fish, but that didn't matter to Peter. He wished his dad could catch some fish now. Anything to cheer him up.

After a moment, he was close enough to listen. He heard his mom say something about a lady smoking a cigar but that didn't make any sense. He listened harder.

He realized they were talking about Rector Hanna from the church and some appointment. Peter liked the lady preacher a lot, wished his parents would take him down there more. He hoped there wasn't something bad happening with the priest or somebody else. People talked about church when folks died, like when his grandfather had passed away three years ago, when Peter was ten. Peter didn't know much about death, except that it seemed pretty final. He didn't feel the need to know more than that.

Abruptly, his parents stopped talking. Peter scampered back to his own room, jumped into the bed. He covered himself up, pulled the sheet over his head and lay still. Now it was silent, except for his own hushed breathing. Still as the mountains when the two of them were camping. Twinges of fear went through him, like little birds flying by his window, little sparrows of troubles he just couldn't shoo away. Even so, he went back to sleep thinking about rainbow trout rising on the lake at sunset.

Chapter 2

The roof of All Souls Episcopal Church peaked like the prow of a wide ship plying the waves. Inside, light from the stained-glass window beamed in bright colored patches onto the red clay tile floor. Barry and Anne sat down in the front pew, across the communion rail from the sanctuary. She folded her hands in her lap and he picked up a hymnal.

Barry knew he was on the hot seat and his palms were damp. Reflexively, he set the book down and sat on his fingertips. Anne's clear brown eyes above high cheek bones gazed at him, expectant. Just a touch of make-up, a hint of rouge. She wore a purple silk blouse instead of the expected clerical black, the severe white collar suprisingly provocative to Barry this close up.

"I'm glad we're finally getting the chance to know each other," Anne said. Her smile said how able she was to accommodate whatever Barry might care to share.

"Thank you for the time, but I really don't know where to start." He ran his fingers through his hair, then captured the hand with his other and held it captive in his lap.

"How are things with the family?" she suggested.

Barry glanced at the colorful window, imagined the summer sun baking his navy blue BMW in the parking lot. He wished he were anywhere but here.

"Martha and I are having a problem with sex. Ever since things started getting crazy at work."

"You still at the gas and electric company?"

"I've been on benefits for about a month, but I could be going back soon, I don't know."

"'Benefits' is what, half pay?"

"Full salary, up to six months."

"Nice. Maybe I should ask you for pledge." She smiled. "What does going back depend on?"

"Me, I guess. My doctor put me on Prozac and told me to take some time off to think things over. Decide if it was worthwhile to go back to the grind."

"You might not go back?"

Barry explained the company's early retirement offer, how it met many of his financial goals.

"You're lucky to have options. Those are more choices than most people get in a lifetime. Surely you're not complaining."

"It's just that there's a price to pay for going back to work." He told her about the chaos on the job, how it had been his task to hold people together. "Next thing I knew, it was me in pieces. If I go back, maybe I'll fall apart again."

"Sometimes we have to fall apart a little to get ourselves back together. It's OK to ask for help when you really need it."

Barry took a deep breath, then exhaled, puffing his cheeks out. "With the Prozac, things got better right away, but my doctor suggested the time off to deal with issues."

"Sounds like you're getting good advice. What sort of issues?"

"Guilt mostly. About Martha. She's getting older and I just don't feel attracted any more. I've been thinking about other women, younger women, like those around the office."

"I'd be more worried if you *didn't* have those kind of thoughts. Have you done anything about it?"

"No!" Barry caught his breath. "But I thought about it."

"Yes?"

He told her about a younger woman at work who had invited him to her apartment for coffee.

"Did you go?"

"I wanted to." Barry was glad for the difference between Anne and his doctor. Her directness was challenging and refreshing at the same time.

She looked at him caringly. "I need to ask a question about your sex life. Do you think that would be all right?"

"There isn't much to talk about."

"Do you masturbate with these women in mind?"

His face grew hot. He imagined his cheeks turning crimson. *Maybe her directness isn't such a good idea after all-* he thought.

"Actually, I don't masturbate. Never got the habit."

Anne looked at him puzzled then said, "I'll give you the benefit of the doubt, but that's quite unusual. Does Martha know?"

"No! Why would I talk to her about that?"

Anne's face looked reasonable, composed. "She probably assumes that you do it occasionally. She might not realize you have a problem."

"The problem is I'm tense and stressed out when I come home from work. I'm not *interested* in sex."

"I'm getting mixed messages, Barry. First of all, it's very normal under stress to lose the sex drive. I think I can assure you it will return when you relax a bit. At least we know it worked at one time. Peter is evidence of that."

"Right," Barry grinned.

"Secondly, if you decide not to masturbate it's your choice. So long as your plumbing is in order."

"I believe it is, thank you." He he frowned. "I worry about Peter. He and I were always very close, but lately we don't do much. He sits around watching TV, won't play sports, none of the things we used to do."

"He's probably as worried about you as you are about him."

"I've tried to talk with him about sex, but he won't listen to me."

"Maybe he's shy. Many boys are. Shy around their fathers, and more so with their mothers."

"Martha won't do it. She says it's my job."

"Well, I tend to agree with her. But if you can't rise to the occasion, somebody's got to do the job." She gave a wry smile, but a pang of embarrassment jabbed him.

"It's guilt. Guilt about sex, guilt about the job. I feel like that guy in the Christmas Carol. Like I've wrapped chains around myself."

"I like what you said, that you've wrapped them around yourself. Jacob Marley came to warn Scrooge about his fate. But Marley was dead," Anne said slowly. "You're not. And while you're alive you can make changes. That was Marley's message."

"I feel chained to the marriage. I worry that it might be over."

"Do you want it to be over?"

"No, not for a minute . . . Well, maybe sometimes."

"Lots of my parishioners have those thoughts. So far, you haven't done anything wrong. Give yourself some credit." She unfolded and folded her hands. Barry noticed a slender gold ring with blue lapis inlay. "Was there anything else you wanted to talk to me about?"

He felt more relaxed now, like maybe it wasn't such a big deal after all. "It's just this dream I had last night."

"You want to tell me about it?"

Barry took several deep gulps of air, felt composed. Slowly he told her the details of his fever dream.

" . . . and if I do the wrong thing the whole world will come to an end."

After a pause, she asked when he started having the dream.

He told her about the headaches and fevers he began having when he was thirteen, how the worst of them coincided with the dreams.

"Peter's 13 now, isn't he?" she asked.

Barry nodded.

"What did the doctor say?"

"Thought it might be alergies, but after awhile they just went away."

"But the dream stayed?"

"Yeah."

"You dream this very many times?"

"I haven't dreamed it in maybe twenty years . . . until last night."

"Any other details about the dream?"

He ran through details again, his memories becoming more precise with each telling. When he closed his eyes, he caught glimpses of dark pictures.

"What do you feel like is happening?" she asked.

His lips stiffened. "If I move one iota, the train will derail and everything will fly apart."

"That's pretty powerful stuff," she said after a pause.

"So you think it's important?"

"A dream can show us where we are in our lives. Images manifest our guilt and fears, our joy as well. Your dream certainly says a lot."

"I thought the train might represent death, or the world coming to an end."

She chuckled. "It might feel like that, but dream symbols usually stand for something much closer to home, more tangible . . . It could be you need to do more with this dream. There's a method I've used before. Try to come up with more details. Write them down, then free-associate. Write it all down, even the most insignificant thing."

"Kind of like a mind map," he said.

"Exactly. You're looking for the thing that clicks, the thing that makes you go, 'Aha!' When you have that, you know you're on to something."

Barry saw Anne glance at her watch. Tension had settled in his legs, which ached from the cramps the night before. He realized he was sitting on his fingers again.

"I have another appointment in a little while," she said. "Would you like to talk again next week?" She stood to go.

Barry was relieved that she didn't mention prayer. "Next week would be fine," he said, standing. "Same time?"

"Maybe we could start a little earlier next time," she said. "We might have time to pray. Meanwhile, do your homework. Write it down. It could be nothing, but it might be something." Her eyes were kind, concerned.

Barry scowled as the thought rang in his head like a signal bell - *What in the world can that train be?*

Anne put her hand on his arm as she walked him to his car. Then, in the middle of the parking lot, she gave him a hug. He felt her wiry frame, strong and hard through the thin fabric of her shirt, her small breasts.

He felt an unaccustomed sense of peace as she waved and said good-bye. Starting his car to drive home, he told himself he didn't care what she was into, she was all right in his book. He gunned the motor before putting it into gear, couldn't wait to get home and tell Martha all about it.

At the traffic light next to the church, Barry saw the long line of commuters heading away from Point Loma and the Navy base. He imagined the rush hour traffic jamming the usually placid surface streets and made an impulsive swerve to the left, against the flow of cars onto Catalina Boulevard. It was smooth sailing past the lines of jammed workers headed home, past the entrance to the college he'd attended in the 70's, and out onto the base. A sentry with white gloves waved unceremoniously as he went through the gate. *Time for everybody to go home* - Barry thought.

To both sides of the macadam road, the white stakes of Fort Rosecrans National Cemetery stretched away, to the east towards the city of San Diego and to the right towards Sunset Cliffs and the shining blue Pacific. Now there was virtually no traffic, but a steady ration of bicyclists and joggers sweating proudly in their afternoon rituals. The sun was hot and Barry hit the button to roll down his windows. A fresh breeze blew off the sea and through the passenger compartment with a salty tang. Mixed in at one point was a hint of sewage from the treatment plant located above the cliffs. *That's a good, earthy smell* - Barry thought, *like agar.*

He avoided paying the parking fee at Cabrillo Monument by taking the right hand fork down the Point to the new lighthouse. The winding, two-lane track reminded him of college, of the road to the dormitories he used to walk up for breakfast at the cafeteria. He'd come a long way since then, he mused, so why was he still here, still hanging around? The Cliffs had always represented a kind of energy vortex to him, from Madame Tingley's Theosophical Society at the beginning of the century to the crazy band of gypsies that had populated his college days. Madame Tingley had built an idyllic estate on the edge of the world, complete with a Greek ampitheater and exotic plants from all over the globe. She had invited masters from India to form a Raja Yoga academy on the grounds, the first wave of a spiritual invasion that would eventually become absorbed by the Hippie culture fifty years later. In those days of revolution, Barry had been among the ones with long hair and tie dyed clothes who roamed the Cliffs in search of secluded spots to smoke reefer and trip out on LSD.

Even then, the power and technology of the U. S. Navy had dominated the high ground, warding off any potential military invader while its labyrinths of pill boxes and tunnels stretched out underground in Faustian menace. Today the Navy shared the point with tourists, sanitation engineers, and seals. Even the dolphin tanks, where secret experiments had been carried out in front of God and everybody, were gone. Barry parked in the lot above the rock beach that was now a nature preserve and shut the car off.

A few day trippers meandered between their rental cars and the cliff walk. An attractive young Japanese couple, took turns photographing each other. Barry thought about offering to snap a shot of both of them, but decided to keep to himself. He sat there and watched the surf roll, long empty walls of green and sparkling sunlight, felt the slight rocking of the car in the wind, twiddled with the radio until the golden light of sunset formed a path out to the kelp beds and the horizon beyond. He felt empty of all thought now, drawn like a moth to the light of the sun, drowning in the roar of the pounding waves.

After awhile, a thought occurred to him: *When I die, I'll have Martha scatter my ashes out there.*

Then he remembered his visit with Anne and his family waiting for him. Hurriedly, he turned the key to leave.

Oh, shit - he thought, *I'm late.*

Fever Dream

Chapter 3

Peter watched Batman slide down into the driver's seat of the Batmobile. He wished there weren't so many Batman actors. He couldn't get used to all the different ones. And Robin was a wimp. Any decent villain should be able to kick his ass.

Peter sat in the leather easy-chair with his feet up, in the living room of the sprawling ranch-style house built on the green hillside of Mount Helix. *Sprawling.* That's what his mom called it, in what was left of her Texas drawl. He glanced out the blinds at dusky shadows spread across the lawn. Almost dark. He heard the car laboring in low gear up the hill, wishing it was his dad's dream car, a British racing green MG-A that Peter would get his hands on when he turned sixteen, instead of their boring blue BMW. Late at night, Peter would imagine himself sitting in the soft leather bucket, working the smooth gears in and out, his toes stretched to the clutch pedal. *Grow six more inches and it'll be a cinch* - Peter thought, then remembered to add - *in my dreams.*

He heard the backdoor open. Dad was home. Peter hollered, "Hello," and hit the mute button on the remote control. After a few seconds, his dad stuck his head into the living room, smiled in a tired kind of way.

"How's it goin', Pete?" he asked, his voice positively wasted.

"Fine," Peter answered. *How's that for non-committal* - he told himself. He liked that word, *non-committal*, ever since he'd read it in a book and looked it up. Now he used it all the time, in his head, if not in actual words. "How was your meeting?" he asked. *Gingerly.* That was another word he liked.

"Interesting but boring, if you know what I mean. Made me want to go back to work again. But . . ."

"You've got to follow doctors' orders," Peter interrupted, finishing the line he'd heard a thousand times. "Mom called and said she'd be late again," he added. "Something about a client from out-of-town." He locked eyes with his dad and made a sad face. "Doesn't she have any customers who are from *in* town?"

"Both you and I wish," Dad said, as he stepped into the living room. He tripped over Peter's Cloud Nine longboard, the skateboard rolling into the coffee table leg, luckily not leaving a mark.

Peter gulped. He'd forgotten to put the board away, and he now he blushed.

Damn - he thought, *the last thing I want is to get Dad angry.* Not that he was mean or anything, but sometimes Dad got so angry there was no telling *what* he would do. *Depressed*, he called it. And when that happened, there was nothing Peter could do to cheer him up.

"Sorry about the board, Pop."

"No sweat, kid. I'm too pooped to get mad."

Dad slumped on the couch and turned his eyes to the big-screen TV where Batman and Robin were having a silent conversation. Then there was an explosion. Mr. Freeze was at it again. Peter couldn't figure out how Arnold could have got hooked into doing such a dumb movie. He switched back to Dad. Something major was bothering him, had to be. He just hoped it wasn't something Peter had messed up, like his parents' whole lives.

He turned the sound back on, but now he was bored. He'd seen it five or six times. He waited for his dad to make the next move.

Suddenly Dad put his hand on his forehead like he was taking his own temperature. "Shit," he said.

Peter cringed, as frozen as a victim in one of Arnold's freeze rays. He wanted to ask Dad what was wrong, but he couldn't move his mouth. He looked at his dad's eyes, noticed how red and tired-looking they were. He seemed to be holding his breath. Peter managed to speak.

"You want to watch something else? There's a ball game on." Dad loved baseball, but that was a sore subject these days, too. If only Peter had gone out for Pony League. If he'd played baseball maybe Dad wouldn't have gone off the deep end.

Dad just sat there. Finally, he said, "No." That's all, just no.

Peter punched a button on the remote and the screen changed. The familiar voices of the guys at the game came on and Quilvio Veras made a nice pivot at second to complete a double play. They ran off the field and it went to commercial.

"Damn it!" Dad jumped up.

Peter recoiled, lifting his arm to block a smack if it came. Quickly, he recovered and turned off the TV. Dad was on the move, and Peter got up to follow him. In the kitchen, he watched him carefully. Dad stomped over to the counter. Drawers opened and slammed. Slivers, their cat, backed away from her water bowl and tore out the open window to the back yard. Then the silverware drawer came away in Dad's hand and forks, spoons and knives clattered across the floor.

"God damn it!" Dad shouted, throwing the drawer to the floor with a crash. He stood with his fists on his waist, his head bent.

Peter stood in the doorway, waited to see what would come next, prepared to run. The kitchen had been pretty clean before, except for an empty soda can and a granola bar wrapper. Now it looked like a shipwreck, and Peter felt like the cabin boy about to get the blame. His dad turned towards him, as if noticing him for the first time, his face dark with anger. Peter felt shivers run through his body.

"Why isn't anything ready for dinner? You sit here all afternoon like a couch potato, I suppose you want me to take you to McDonald's now."

His words tore through Peter like machine gun bullets. Riddled, Peter backed away, turned down the hall and ran.

Inside his room, he shut the door, careful not to slam it, and got down on the carpet behind the bed. His Sony Walkman CD player and headphones were where he'd left them. He stabbed the button and shut his eyes as the Beatles' Magical Mystery Tour rolled into his ears. He imagined himself in a crowd lining up for a bus ride anywhere but here. He felt the rush of blood to his face, tears stinging his eyes. This was his dad's music, maybe it could save him. As the jangly piano music faded, he tried to imagine himself alone on a hill with the world spinning around. Peter Sumner, the fool on the hill. His heart still thumped in his chest, but his hands had stopped shaking. He took a peek over the bed.

His dad stood there, leaning his back against the door, eyes shut. He seemed calm enough. Peter took the headphones off and stood up.

"Dad? You OK?" He heard him take a deep breath, then blow it out slowly. His eyes opened and he looked to Peter as if he hadn't slept for a week. He felt tired just looking at him.

"No, son, I'm not OK. And I owe you an apology."

"Nah, that's all right. I know you're having a tough time. I'm just sorry I made it tougher." Peter loved him, but hated being around when he lost control. And that could be anytime.

Dad knelt by the bed, put his arms out towards Peter. "None of this is your fault. I want you to believe me."

Peter kept quiet. He didn't want to tell Dad that he didn't believe him, not for a second. He wanted to believe his dad, so bad his stomach ached. He shoved his doubts deeper, handled his embarrassment by chewing his lip. He'd seen Arnold do that in a movie, and he had nothing what so ever to be embarrassed about. Until Mr. Freeze.

Peter walked to the other side of the bed, sat down next to Dad and gave him a hug.

"Sure, Dad," he lied. "I believe you."

He felt his dad's arms around him as hard and strong as Arnold's must feel, and smelled that hint of aftershave that always stayed on Dad's shirts, even after they came out of the laundry. Some things never went away.

"That's great," Dad said. He stood up, towering a whole head above Peter.

Peter looked up at him, wondering if he'd ever start that growth spurt his dad kept talking about. He willed his hands not to shake, his knees to stop trembling. If he could only will his legs to grow.

"What d'ya say we go out and find a pizza?" Dad asked. "I could use some pepperoni."

"Fine," Peter said, remembering the pimple that had appeared on his cheek the day before. Mom told him greasy foods make pimples, that he was going to have to start watching what he ate. He remembered thinking - *Great, another thing to be careful about!*

He followed his dad out of the room and down the hall. One wall was covered with family photographs, the other held a picture by Marc Chagal. His mom called it a *litho*. She said the painter was an *Impressionist*. Peter just thought he drew like a kid and that's why he liked him. He looked at picture of the donkey flying around in the air, something he'd wondered about a thousand times. Nothing adults did made sense to him.

In the kitchen, on the way to the garage, he noticed his father had picked up all the silverware and straightened up.

I wish I could get stuff done that fast! It looked like nothing had happened in there at all. Quickly, he went out, making sure the door was locked behind him. Then he shut the door tight on his memories.

Fever Dream

Chapter 4

When he awoke, Barry couldn't wait to tell Martha about the new dream. He thought about his tantrum in the kitchen the previous night, but the guilt that had weighed him down the night before had vanished. He was sure this reprieve was God's way of telling him everything was going to be all right.

Martha was in the garden in her nightgown, watering roses. He crept up behind her and barely avoided a squirt of the hose as she fended him off.

Sometimes she grins just like a little girl - he thought.

"Missed me!" He approached carefully to give her a hug, which she allowed.

"You're in a good mood this morning." She hadn't put her makeup on yet but her natural beauty matched the roses, only slightly past their prime. He kissed her cheek. "To what do I owe the pleasure?"

"Martha, I just had the most amazing dream." He couldn't begin to keep the excitement from his voice. "It was as vivid as the Wizard of Oz, I swear. It showed me everything that I ever was, and who I am today."

"And who might that be?" she asked.

"I swear, I feel like Ebenezer Scrooge on Christmas Day!"

"Well, stop swearing and tell me more. Or shall I give *you* a Christmas goose?" She tried to reach around him but he skirted away.

"No, really. It was all about when I was a kid. There was this small town just like where I grew up. Elm trees everywhere, just like home. And kids on bikes whizzing up and down the hill, riding to school on a two-lane highway, zipping right past all the cars. I was worried at first, but the kids were stronger and more confident than any kids I ever saw. Then car loads of Boy Scouts going on a camping trip with their dads. Not where you spend the night in cabins, but a real backwoods experience."

Martha grinned. "Sounds like a blast, but isn't the ground awfully hard?" She rubbed her back in fun.

"And then I was in the school house, with the principal. We *sang* at each other, a musical comedy number. Solving all the problems of the the educational system on the spot. Then all the teachers got together to say good-bye and they got naked and paraded around in a conga line."

"Sweet Jesus!"

"But it was wholesome and good and joyful. Nothing sordid about it."

"Who were you with in this conga line?" Martha asked, stifling a laugh. "Do I need to worry?"

"No, no. And then I was in somebody's kitchen having dessert and there were cookies and pastries, all sugary and glittery. I swear they glittered like sparklers, turning gold and green and red . . ."

"There you go swearing again."

He waved her off. "And they gave me a pair of mukluks, like the ruby slippers in the Wizard of Oz, only they were emerald green. When I put them on I felt just like I was in heaven. The next thing I knew, I was waking up in my own bed and I hadn't missed a thing. Everything I want and need in my life is right here as close as my own bed. The whole world begins right here, with God smiling down on us all!"

He gazed deep into Martha's eyes and smiled. He'd never felt such a sense of peace and well-being.

Euphoria - he told himself, *this is euphoria.*

"Mukluks, eh?" Martha said. "Instead of ruby slippers. Must be a guy thing."

"I've got an idea," he said. "I'm going to take a trip. It will be great. Me and Peter will go to my home town. I've never been back and I'm dying to show him all the things I did as a kid."

He saw Martha's face darken.

"What's the matter?"

"You can't just go off galivanting around the country," she said. "You're sick. You're on disability benefits and I'm sure they have some rule about it."

"Who cares about that? I don't care about a few days' pay. Besides, who's going to know? I don't have to report anything, I can just go. And if anybody asks, I'll say I went to visit my mother."

"Your mother," she said. "For Chrissake. That's what I feel like these days. You walk out of your job and now you want to go flying all over the country to find your roots. Well, it's not going to happen."

Barry couldn't believe she could take such a callous view.

"What are you talking about? It's just a couple of days. Besides, it will be good for me and Peter."

"Why drag Peter into this? It isn't *his fantasy*," she flung the last word like it was a curse.

"I'm going to do it, Martha. You'll see. It will be all right. In fact, it will be better than all right. It will be wonderful. We'll go to a Cubs game at Wrigley Field, visit the Museum of Science and Industry. See the place where I grew up."

"Wake up, Barry. That's the last thing your son wants. Don't you know anything about him at all?"

"You'll see." He strode across the lawn, feeling like Zeus. "I'm going to make reservations."

"You better not!" She let him have it with the hose full blast.

He slid across the porch and ducked in the door. "It's going to be great!"

Peter looked at Dad and felt his mouth drop. "Oh, no. No, no. You've got to be kidding," he said. "You told me yourself Chicago is like Hell in summer."

"Forget what I said. This is the age of air conditioning. It's everywhere! In cars, at the hotel, even church."

"You mean we have to go to church?" Going to church on vacation was too much like school.

They were having breakfast in the kitchen, talking over glasses of orange juice. Peter picked up his spoon and took a disgusted bite of cereal. Sunshine came through the open window, bounced off the sink and glittered on the counter. *It's hot here, too -* he reflected. Besides, he liked going places with Dad, as long as he didn't go crazy and yell. And he'd never done *that* on a trip, yet. Peter chewed his Frosted Flakes and thought about it.

When he looked up, Dad had the phone in his hand. Now he was speaking to someone. "Yes, I'd like to make two reservations to Chicago for this afternoon."

Peter couldn't believe it. "No, Dad! Wait a minute!"

He held his hand over the receiver "Come on, Peter. It will be great!"

"But, *Dad!*" He saw Dad's look and gave up. He'd simply wanted to tell him that he could buy tickets cheaper over the Internet. His dad didn't trust computers, but he didn't know all that much about them either. Peter was an expert. He munched his cornflakes thoughtfully while his dad finished on the phone. *It couldn't be all bad. We could visit Wrigley field and see a game. Maybe Sammy Sosa would hit a home run. I might even get to catch the ball!*

By the time Dad finished on the phone, Peter was starting to get excited about the whole thing. He even allowed himself a half smile.

"So that's it. We leave this afternoon at four o'clock." Dad had a big, wide smile, what grown-ups call a *shit-eating grin.* They were so weird!

"I had plans, you know," Peter mentioned.

"What plans?"

"Sit around watching HBO, wishing we could be up in the mountains fishing." Peter's grin grew half an inch.

"Hey, no problem, Sport. I can find us a motel that has HBO. You can still wish we were in the mountains. But I thought you didn't like fishing."

Peter's cheeks flushed, and he fought his embarrassment. "Nah," he said. "That was last year. This year, it's going to be different."

Dad gave him a long look, then spoke softly. "Different, huh? You want things to be different? So do I. And I'll do my best to make it happen."

"OK, Dad," Peter said, looking at his cereal. *So much for words* - he thought. *Dad always says the right thing, then does something else.*

Just then, Mom walked in. She had a look of determination which she turned on Peter.

"Well, I hope you talked him out of it," she said.

Peter shrugged, stayed silent.

She looked back and forth between them. "Two against one, 'eh?" She shook her head in resignation. "So that's the way it's going to be. Well, I don't have time to argue about it now. I gotta get ready for work."

She went down the hall to the bedroom. Peter listened carefully, waiting for the door to slam. Silence.

He looked at Dad and smiled again. "I guess we're going to Chicago."

Martha stuck her head into the kitchen. "Barry, I need to speak with you a minute."

He knew he was in trouble. She was dressed in a lime green jacket over jet black trousers and a white silk blouse, and looked ready to kill. He didn't envy the customers who had to resist her today. She'd done her face expertly, as always, eye shadow accenting just perfect, bringing out her natural color, but hell, what did he know about make up? He knew when she looked great.

But behind the rouge, she was dead earnest.

They went back into their bedroom and she closed the door.

"Barry, I'm going to say this as plain as I know how. You are not taking our son back to Chicago on some wild goose chase."

"I've made up my mind."

"Well, you just unmake it. I've got a bad feeling about this."

"Martha, it's like the dream was an invitation from the gods. I've just *got* to go!"

"More like an invitation for disaster."

"Oh, come on now," he said turning his back to her, looked down at the bed. "What could possibly go wrong? We're both big boys now."

"'Big boys' is right. One of you ought to be acting like an adult."

Barry's sense of well-being vanished and he felt anger. "Just how do you plan to stop me? Are you going to withhold sex from me? Maybe you'll cancel all my credit cards. Well, in case you didn't notice, Martha, I am a grown up and I don't need to prove it to you."

She pointed her finger at him, held his gaze square between the eyes.

"Barry," she said, "I've got too many important meetings today to stay home and argue with you about this." She softened her voice. "I want you to promise."

Chapter 5

It was a view of Chicago Barry had never seen before, and felt chills as he watched it unfold. The plane landed at O'Hare Field by dropping into the sunset from out over Lake Michigan. It was like dipping into a huge cauldron of melted gold. Below them, rooftops cast dark shadows in the jet's wake as they flew past. At touchdown, the screech of tires and the roar of jets backing up filled the cabin, which shook like a popcorn popper for about six seconds, then settled down as they made a smooth turn at the end of the runway. Barry looked at his watch. Eight o'clock, local time. Right on target.

He smiled at his son, who had his whole head practically sticking out the window. Barry tapped Peter's shoulder. "We're still alive. At least I think so."

Peter turned. He had a big grin, but didn't act excited. "Yeah," he said. "I guess it's pretty cool." His eyes were twinkling with happiness. That was enough for Barry.

Working the airport crowds was more difficult than Barry had anticipated. Besides the usual commuters, planes were filled with vacationers and the terminal flowed with people. Finally retrieving their single suitcase, Barry led them to the rental car counter, which was four deep in customers. He looked at Peter, who didn't seem to mind, then took his place in line.

"This sucks," Peter said, standing next to him with a hand on their luggage.

"Big time," he said. "It's a time to learn patience. My dad taught me."

"You and Grandpa?" Peter asked.

"He used to race cars, back in the sixties. He took me and my mom to a race one time, back in Texas. I was twelve. We had to drive back all night, towing the race car behind the station wagon. In this little town, about three in the morning, the tow hitch started to pull away and we had to stop. I remember the town was a plague of locusts. There were crickets and grasshoppers of every size and shape. Squashed on the sidewalks, jammed in the windshield wipers, all over the windows, smashed bugs. I could hear the rest singing everywhere. It was spooky. But I remember sitting on the curb next to my dad wondering what we were going to do and he said it was time to learn patience. Those were the longest hours, waiting there for the gas station to open up at dawn so we could fix the tow hitch, but they passed somehow. Dad welded steel onto the bumper of the race car to brace the tow bar, and fixed it. And I learned patience."

Barry had been moving along with the other customers in line and now was standing at the rental counter. He smiled at the customer service rep, a pretty blonde woman in her twenties who looked like she could really use a coffee break. After a few minutes and a credit card swipe, the deal was done. Barry and Peter headed for their car.

Peter watched the lights all around them while Dad fidgeted with the radio. Pretty soon, Dad had the station he wanted. Voices sang from the speakers, *Double You El Ess, in Chicago. Channel Eighty-nine.* Peter wished his dad would leave the music to him, let him find a decent station. It looked like a pretty good radio, but AM sucked.

"There we go, Sport," Dad said. "That's the station I used to listen to when I was a kid. I remember a DJ named Dick Biondi calling some guy on the phone and ordering a chocolate pizza. I remember *The Monster Mash,* and they used to play these stories punctuated with lines from all different songs, like some ganster movie where Johnny gets shot and he sings *I don't wanna cry.* Sometimes I used to listen all night."

"That's *great*, Dad," Peter said faceciously. He hated when Dad called him "Sport". It made him feel like a dog. And the music on this station sucked. It was all he could to keep from putting his fingers in his ears, so he concentrated on watching cars. Up ahead, red lights blazed bright on the Expressway, as Dad called it. Not a freeway, like in California, but a toll road where you had to pay at booths along the way. *What a hassle* - Peter thought, *having to stop and pay every few miles. Why don't we just pull over and stop every half hour? Kind of like going to sleep every night. What the heck was the point?*

The brake lights got brighter and closer, and Peter noticed a long cloud of smoke hovering over the car roofs. After a few minutes in the stop and start traffic, Peter could see a car ablaze, completely engulfed in flames. It looked like it had been a Volkswagen Rabbit, maybe, but the sides of the car were bending and melting in the intense heat. Bright orange tongues of fire danced ten feet high.

"Wow," Dad said.

"Cool," said Peter.

"Never make fun or laugh at another person's misfortune," his dad admonished.

Peter felt his ears burn with embarrassment. "I *know*, Pop," he said.

A short distance away, a small knot of people huddled near another car, and a police cruiser with lights flashing pulled over. Peter got to watch the fire for about ten minutes, long enough to see a bright yellow fire engine arrive and douse what was left of the car in foam. It looked like a washing maching overflowed onto the side of the road, spilling into the traffic lanes. Then they were past, and the highway was clear.

Peter felt the car accelerate and turned back to look at his dad. A grim look had fastened itself to him, as if somebody had pulled a stocking mask over his face and pulled it tight from behind.

"What's the matter, Dad?"

"I remember a picture I saw in the newspaper when I was a kid. It was on this road. Some lady was on her knees next to her car, crying her eyes out, her arms out as though somebody could help her. On the road in front of her was one little cowboy boot, all crumpled. Her little boy had fallen out of the back door while they were driving and got killed. Nothing about this road looks familiar to me anymore, I mean it's been more than thirty years, but I still remember that picture like I'm looking at it up close. And that lady's face."

"Don't worry, Pop. I've got my seatbelt on," Peter said. "Didn't the little boy have a seatbelt?"

"No," he said. "Nobody had them back then. It was like way back in the Stone Age, or the Ice Age, or something."

"*Right*," Peter said, as his dad tromped on the gas. The little rental had some guts after all.

They pulled into the Holiday Inn at Wheaton, Illinois, a set of low buildings that still looked new. To Peter, they looked like two concrete layer cakes set side by side. They left the car under the overhang and walked across the lobby to the reception desk. A few sets of couches and chairs were arranged on one side of the long room, around a fireplace with no fire and a TV set that was on with nobody watching. Something on the screen exploded, drawing Peter's eyes like a magnet. He saw an aircraft carrier and some jets taking off. Then they were at the counter.

The man behind the reception desk had a flat face. Dull eyes behind wire-rimmed specktacles. His sandy hair was turning gray at the temples and his lips were thin, a smile that seemed attached by rubber bands to his ears. His voice had a twang to it and Peter realized that was the Chicago accent. *God* - Peter thought, *if we lived here I'd have to sound like that.*

Business only took a minute. Dad told the guy the license number off the rental and let him swipe the credit card. *I can do that job* - Peter thought. *That's a cinch.* Room 322 was waiting. They left the lobby and pulled the car around to the other side of the main building. Dad got the suitcase out of the trunk, but Peter insisted on rolling it across the parking lot to the elevator.

"Don't they have bellboys here?" Peter asked.

"This is a *motel*," his dad answered. "In a *hotel* you get a bellboy. A motel you fend for yourself. Unless you're an old lady or something. You got that suitcase all right?"

"No problem, Dad," Peter huffed, lifting it out the elevator door into the hall. "This ain't heavy. I could carry it all the way." He rolled it on its little wheels like a shopping cart. "Heck, a girl could roll this thing."

"That's why they make 'em with wheels, son."

They stood in front of room 322. Dad inserted the key card through the magnetic lock and swung the door open. With a flourish, he handed Peter a key of his own.

"For you, my good man," he said. Peter stuck the card in his back pocket like it was no big deal, but he felt proud. And he liked being called a man.

They went in and Peter took a quick inventory. Two double beds, a TV, a writing desk, a low dresser, and a small table with two chairs. Two telephones, one on the writing desk and one between the beds. The air conditioner hummed like a waterfall and cool, dry air hit him in the face like soft fingers. French doors led to a balcony that overlooked what? A swimming pool? No, he saw only a small park with walkways between the two buildings. About half the lights in the other building were on. To one side were the lights of Wheaton,

34

low office buildings, shadows of tree tops. Nothing to write home about.

Peter thought about the motel they'd stayed at coming down out of the Sierra's. It had been a hundred and five in the valley, the sweat evaporating off your face before it had a chance to bead up. They'd been all grimy from four nights up by the lake, like a couple of old sourdough prospectors. Dad hadn't shaved and was all prickly. Peter couldn't wait for his own whiskers to start. Right off, Peter had gone swimming, then walked along the stream that ran through the landscaped grounds. He was dry before he got back to the room and didn't need a towel, except for his swim suit. Later, Dad had showed him how long he could hold his breath, swimming two times across the pool underwater. Peter could barely make it one time. Except this year he could probably make it half way on the second lap. Part of him was itching to try.

"Let's hit the pool, Dad," he said, excited.

"Whoa, hold on there. It's late and we haven't had supper yet. What do you say we go down to the restaurant and get us a steak?"

"I'm not hungry," Peter explained. "I want to swim."

"Not tonight," Dad said, kind of snapping at him. Right away Peter understood. His dad was tired. It didn't do any good arguing with him when he was tired, he'd only get mad. He sure didn't want any yelling in a damn motel.

Peter went over and rolled onto one of the beds. "I got this one!" he said. He bounced and flopped around like a fish on dry land. His dad chuckled.

"OK, buddy. I'll take the other one. How about that steak?"

"Aw, Dad. I really don't feel like going to any restaurant. How about we call for room service?"

"Room service always costs extra. You pay for the priviledge of eating in your room."

"Yeah," Peter said. "Your point?"

"Well, I'm paying the bill, so I ought to get to decide."

Now it was Peter's turn to get grumpy. "I can pay my own way. I brought some of my own money." Peter was a saver, normally. He had paid for his own computer last year with money he saved himself. And he still had plenty of money stashed away for college, money from birthdays and Christmas, from his grandparents, aunts and uncles. He didn't throw money around, but tonight he wanted room service. He looked his dad in the eye and turned on his will power. Then he stuck his tongue out and Dad cracked a smile.

"OK, OK. You win this time. Room service it is," his father gave in.

They discussed who should make the call and what they wanted to eat. Peter called down for two club sandwiches with French Fries and a Personal Pan pepperoni pizza, while his dad went down the hall to find the ice machine and some Cokes. This gave Peter a chance to investigate the television and movie channels. To his dismay, the remote control was tethered to the night stand between the two beds and would barely reach three feet in any direction. But HBO was free, as was Cinemax, and there was a menu with movies on demand, nine bucks a pop. Maybe this wasn't going to be a total loss of a trip. He looked at the categories and listings, including Adults Only, and saw several titles he was interested in. Peter didn't give a damn about watching movies with sex. He much preferred a good spy thriller. There were sexy ladies in those, and that was just OK.

His dad came back in the room.

"Hey," Peter called. "We get this station back home on cable." He had the channel on WGN, whose local commercials had familiarized him with many Chicago businesses even though he lived two thousand miles away. He liked the news people better than the ones from San Diego and it didn't really matter to him that the local stories were about people thousands of miles away. News was like that anyhow.

Dad was fixing Cokes in those short glasses they always give you at motels. At least these were made of glass, so it wasn't a cheesy motel.

They settled in around the small table, their Cokes sweating drops on the sides, and for awhile they didn't speak. The TV blah, blahhed, but Peter wasn't interested, even though it was Charles Bronson. He reached in his shirt and fingered the necklace Mom had given him, a jade arrowhead on a black velvet string. For just a second, he wished she were here, wondered how she was doing, but it was dumb to miss her already. She'd just seen them off at the airport, less than three hours ago. He wasn't some homesick kid anymore.

Things picked up when a knock came at the door. A muffled *Room Service*.

"That was quick," Dad said.

Peter watched the guy come in with a big tray on his shoulder and lay out their meal on the tiny table. Placemats and everything, real napkins wrapped around silverware. Little silver salt and pepper shakers. A quick thought prodded him to pocket them, but that would be stealing and Peter wasn't about to give in to that. Dad shook hands with the guy and Peter noticed him passing a folded up bill for a tip.

That wasn't really necessary, was it? - Peter thought. *Doesn't that guy get paid anyway?* Mom would call it *extravagant*, in her drawl. Especially a fiver. Peter had caught a glimpse of Lincoln's face. He knew money. But Peter put on a smile and shook away his concern. He focused on the food, although he wasn't really hungry at all.

"This looks really good," Peter said, and his dad agreed. They dug in with fervor, passing the salt shaker to each other in turn, and the ketchup bottle once it had got going, for the big steak fries. After his first bite, Peter knew it was going to be all right. *I can get into this* - he told himself. Even the pizza looked good, steamy hot, and for once, Peter didn't get on his own case about his weight.

Towards the end of dinner, they started talking again, in between swallows.

"There's a good movie on Pay-Per-View tonight," Peter pointed out.

"Oh, yeah? What's that?"

"Bond. James Bond." Peter did a good Sean Connery.

His dad wiped a napkin across his lips. "I thought maybe we could go into the city and catch a flick. At one of the big theaters."

"Aw, Dad. We can do that tomorrow, can't we? I really don't feel like driving around anymore tonight."

"Getting tired, Sport?"

Again that name. Peter put on a brave face anyway. He smiled, but he wanted to sulk. "Yeah," he said, "I'm kinda tired." He thought about the Bond film on, that new one he hadn't seen yet. He liked watching Bond films with his dad. To him, it was a guy thing. Back home they had most of the videos, and Peter had read six of the books.

His dad gave him a long, curious look, as if measuring him for some new clothes, or picturing him with different hair cut. "All right," he said slowly. "We can do that."

37

"Great," Peter said. His smile felt genuine again, but he wondered about that look. He tried to relax and poked around with a French Fry in the ketchup.

Maybe I should have ordered dessert - he thought.

Chapter 6

All through supper, Barry had noticed how grown up his son looked. Just the way he held his mouth, the calm concentration of the eyes. Pride swelled in his chest. Yet he felt distant, as though he could not really communicate with the boy. He had so much to tell him, about the trials he had gone through at the Electric Company, about his owns doubts about himself, the despair that changed into a brick wall right in front of his face. He simply could not go any further with his life until he did something about it. Yet he felt so helpless, out of control, unmanageable. For a man who prided himself on handling tough situations and managing people, he had come to the brink of complete failure. At times, he wondered if he would be better off to have followed the impulse to jump out of the sixteen story window at his office. To throw a chair through the glass first, and then follow in a long, arching swan dive.

Peter was the reason he couldn't do it. The last thing in his life he wanted to do was leave behind that kind of legacy for his son. Looking at the boy over a slice of pizza, he faced the strange paradox of feeling so close, so intimate with him, but being unable to share those thoughts and feelings, at a complete loss to account for them, even to himself. That's what Prozac had done for him, given him the ability to move through life without resolving these conflicts, with some sense of detachment. But he wasn't interested in detachment when it came to Peter. He wanted to feel connected.

When they'd finished eating, Barry cleared the remains onto the tray the porter had left on the bed and set them aside on the floor. Then he freshened up their Cokes. He'd given Peter the go ahead to order the Bond movie on the Pay Channel, so he sat down on the bed to unwind. He kicked off his loafers, the ones Peter kept telling him to put dimes in, or at least pennies. Even though he'd been sitting down most of the day, either flying or driving, his feet hurt. Probably swelling up from lack of activity, he thought.

While his son ran through the program on the TV to order the movie, Barry lay back on the bed and loosened his belt. He was full of food, feeling bloated from the French Fries. A dull headache insinuated itself behind his ears, the same place he used to hurt when he was a kid. He thanked God he hadn't had one of *those* headaches since the last time he was in Wheaton, headaches that would never abate until after he had vomitted. That was a long time ago, he mused, more than thirty years. He'd left from O'Hare Field with his family on a plane to San Antonio, Texas, and had never returned until today. All those years of wandering coming back to haunt me, he supposed.

He sat up and stuck his feet back in his shoes.

"I'm going to go down to the lobby for a little while," he said.

Peter looked over at him, concern in his eyes. "Everything all right, Dad?"

"Ahh," he said. "I'm getting a little headache. Think I'll see if I can find some Tylenol downstairs."

"Caffene's good for it. Have another Coke, Pop. The movie will be on in just a second."

"That's OK, Sport. You go ahead without me. I won't be long." Barry got up and shuffled towards the door.

"Aww, Pop. You know the beginning of these movies is always the best part. You're gonna miss it."

He stopped and looked back at his son with a raised eyebrow. "We saw it at the theater a few months ago. It's just the sillouettes of some naked ladies dancing around."

"That was the one before, and it was almost two years ago," the boy reminded him.

"Anyhow, I liked the ones with Sean Connery best."

"At least they don't change heroes every picture like Batman. Connery got old, Pop, like somebody else I know." Youthful sarcasm softened the blow to Barry's pride. "His last one had him kissing Kim Bassinger and it was gross. Imagine if it was an old lady and a young stud. How about Vanessa Redgraves and Tom Cruise making out in Mission Impossible. Would that give you a thrill?"

"Thanks for the image," Barry said, "but I think I can live without it for now. See ya soon."

"OK. It's your loss. See ya."

Barry noted the resignation in the boy's voice, but went out the door anyway.

Peter's a big boy - he thought. *Besides, we're both just tired.* In the hallway, he suddenly felt better, the headache evaporating like a vague memory, and decided to stretch his legs a bit. He headed for the elevator with a light step.

Chapter 7

In the lobby, Barry heard sounds of conversation and laughter coming from the cocktail lounge. He stuck his head in the darkened door and saw tables and chairs for perhaps fifty, but only a handfull of them were occupied. Two men and a woman in a shadowy corner generated most of the talking he had heard. The fat man with the striped tie chose that moment to open his wide mouth and guffaw at some joke Barry didn't catch. The waitress standing by her station at the bar looked over at them and shook her head, pulling a wry grin. The bartender wiped a glass dry with a white towel. Barry headed to the bar and sat down in a leather swivel chair that creaked.

Jake was the bartender, according to the tag on his golf shirt. His arms were muscled and tan, as if he had plenty of time during the day to hit golf balls. He tossed his towel over a shoulder and gave Barry a nod.

"What'll it be, sir?"

"Brandy and ginger ale, please." Barry swung around to face the room. There were television sets in all four corners, mounted up high, a golf match on two of them and twin talking heads on the others. The volume was turned down and music wafted from speakers in the ceiling. Barry recognized Pat Metheny on guitar, played subliminally low. When he turned around again, his drink sweated on a napkin in front of him. Jake stood there smiling.

"Three fifty."

Barry gave him a five out of his pants pocket, turned his attention down the bar to his right. At the end, in a circle of light, a woman with shiny black hair sat with a stir straw connecting her red lips to a tall fruit drink. As he watched, she put down the straw, plucked a cherry by its stem from the drink and inserted it in her mouth. She chewed slowly a few times, then reached in with her manicured fingers, pulled out the stem and set it on the bar. It was tied in a knot.

She looked right at Barry and he half expected her to wink, but she didn't. She just stared straight at him like he wasn't even there, a pretty face, but flat of all emotion. His palms began to sweat.

Jake smacked Barry's change down, startling him.

He managed a grin to match Jake's, pretended everything was fine, and fumbled in his pockets for more bills.

"You sell cigarettes, Jake, is it?" Barry stammered. "I need a pack of smokes."

"Angie!" Jake called to the waitress, who walked over in tall heels and a short skirt.

Angie smiled at Barry. "What do you like?" she asked with a heavy midwest accent.

"What brand," Jake interpreted, flattening the vowel like a Pepsi can under his shoe.

"Marlboro red," Barry blurted. He hadn't smoked in three years, but he hadn't been in a bar since then either.

Angie turned half a pirouette and stepped towards the door on legs that were too young to show the wear and tear of her profession. Strong, farm girl legs, Barry thought, elonogated by the spiked heels. Made her ass firm and round under the skirt, he imagined, as he picked up his ginger ale and sipped.

"You're a strange cat," Jake observed. "Not really a player, are ya?" He wiped another glass. "Don't mind Soupie," he said, jerking a thumb at the lady down the bar. "She does that cherry thing to all the new studs in town."

Barry sputtered and had to put the back of his hand over his mouth to keep the drink from spurting out.

"Soupie?" Barry managed.

"Yeah, my cousin," Jake explained with a wink. "Other wise known as Sophia. You wanna meet 'er? Hey, Soupie, come on over here," he called.

Down the bar, Soupie pointed at her breast, which was partly exposed by a black dress with a neckline like an Alcapulco cliff dive. After more encouragement from Jake, she stood up and began what seemed like a long, perilous journey up the row of stools, her shapely legs rubbing together as she stepped towards him in her mini-dress and pumps. Jake walked down the bar and brought her drink over for her, but Barry's eyes were mostly on her straight black hair, which she pulled back behind one ear with a finger. Barry caught the tropical bouquet of her fruit drink and the musky spice of her perfume at the same time. Jake began introductions, but didn't get too far.

"You got a harmonica?" he asked Barry.

"Huh?"

"A moniker. A name," Jake prodded.

"Barry," he said. "Barry S . . ."

Jake popped up a hand to stop him. "Barry's fine for now," he said. Turning to the lady, he said, "Barry, I'd like you to meet my cousin. Soupie, this is Barry."

"Very pleased to make your acquaintence," she said, her words slightly slurred. She held up a hand as if to be kissed. He expected her to crack a smile, but she didn't.

Barry took her fingers in his, pulled up and down as if milking a tiny cow. "Why do they call you Soupie?" he asked. "If you don't mind me asking."

"Au contraire," the lady said. "I'd be offended if you didn't ask. But first we'd better get another drink. Don!" she shouted, turning to her cousin, who jumped.

"Who's Don?" Barry asked.

"That's me," Jake said. "Ever since we were little, she calls me Don. Something about Don Juan. Don't worry. You can call me Jake."

Angie walked in on her statuesque stilts and plopped a pack of cigarettes on the bar for Barry.

"That'll be four bucks," she said, then turned her attention to Soupie. "Who let you out of your cage?"

"Don said I could come over," Soupie sulked. Suddenly, her face turned to a comic mask of sorrow, black eyebrows and red lips drawn down like a clown.

Angie busted into a laugh. "That's OK. Forget about it," she said, then took the five dollar bill Barry offered from his fingers and went off to see to the party in the corner.

Barry looked at Soupie, whose face was restored to its original deadpan. He caught the twinkle in her eyes as she looked at him, begging him for something, he had no idea what.

"So Soupie," Barry said. "That's an unusual name for a pretty lady."

Her face blossomed into a wide smile, exaggerated beyond any social nicety. "Why, thank you, Barry," she said. "Don, Barry just called me pretty. Don't you think I'm pretty, too?" She batted her eyelids at Jake. "Now how about those drinks?" She switched again to deadpan, an edge of menace on her voice. Jake hurried away, down the bar, began to fidget with the blender, looking for ingredients among the bottles.

"What was that you're having, Soupie? Was that a Mai Tai?" he asked.

"I thought you said you called it a 'bow tie'," Soupie called to him.

As he began to cut up a pineapple, Jake corrected her. "What I said was one more of those and you can go hang yourself."

Barry turned his attention again to Soupie, who had moved closer and was staring into his face, not six inches away. Suddenly, she looked normal, if normal is the word for it, an attractive woman, unselfconscious. Her face was relaxed but dancing with light and life, tiny movements of emotion flickering from her eyes to the corners of her mouth. Barry noticed her makeup, clumsily applied, but highlighting her cheeks, accenting the color of her eyes, which were deep blue. Azure, he thought.

"You gonna offer me a cigarette, or do I have to beg?"

Barry fumbled with the pack.

What the hell am I getting into? - he wondered, his ears burning. Finally, he managed to pull two cigarettes out of the package. She put hers in her mouth, stared at him expectantly. Again, he fumbled, this time with the matches Angie had brought, until he struck one and held it out between them. She leaned to the flame, took a deep drag and held her breath while he lit up. When he was done, she exhaled smoke and blew out the match.

"Way to go, Barry. You light my fire."

Nervously, Barry flicked his cigarette tip at the ashtray. He took a drag and nearly gagged on the smoke. *What the hell am I doing?* - he wondered again.

Jake came back over, set two new drinks on the bar with a flourish.

"That'll be ten bucks," he said, then walked to the waitress station where Angie had returned from the corner table. Barry heard her spit out a drink order rapid fire, which Jake repeated word for word.

"Hey!"

Barry turned back to Soupie. "Hey, what?" he asked with a smile.

Her eyes were travelling over his face, moving her lashes as if they were butterflies flitting from flower to flower. He saw the tiny lines at the corners of her eyes, not quite hidden by makeup, lines that reminded him of his mother. He was beginning to think how odd that was when she spoke again.

"So are you curious?"

"Curious? Yes, I'm curious," he said. Then added, "Curious about what?"

"About my name, silly." She punched him in the arm. Hard. Then she reached for the cherry in her drink and popped it into her mouth.

"Ow!" He said and rubbed his arm, felt a bruise forming. "Yes, yes," he said, not wanting to be hit again. "Tell me about your name. I assumed it was because of your talent for making faces, like Soupy Sales."

"What faces?" she asked, going deadpan again and plucking the cherry stem from her lips, tied in a neat little knot.

He laughed nervously. "Yes, exactly."

"It's because I'm always ready."

"Ready?"

"Yeah, you know. When you're making something and you're not finished yet and somebody asks you if it's soup yet."

"Is it soup yet," Barry repeated blankly.

"Yeah," she answered. "'Cuz I'm ready. I'm always ready."

"Ahh!" Barry agreed, satisfied. Then he ventured, "Ready for what?"

"Anything!" she cried. Again she punched him in the arm, even harder. Then she threw her head back and laughed at the ceiling, her laugh like the sound of bells. Even the fat man in the corner stopped talking and watched her send herself up in stitches. Barry found himself mystified, vibrating with her intensity. After a moment, she calmed down, took a kleenex from her clutch bag and wiped her eyes. Barry was stupefied, wondering what she might do next.

Finally composing herself, she sniffed, dabbed at her nostrils.

"So, Barry, are you ready?" Soupie asked.

Trying to hide his exasperation, Barry pulled a wan smile. "Ready for what?"

"Come on. Let's go." She reached over and raked the inside of his thigh with the tips of her fingernails. He looked down, saw her hand on him and her skirt hiked up above her bare thighs. Her perfume began to overwhelm him and he had a bizarre feeling as if he'd been punched in the stomach. Meanwhile his manhood began to jump to attention.

"Oh, God," he said, the blood draining from his face.

"Come on, lover," she cooed. "I'll be real good to you tonight. All you gotta do is pick up my bar tab."

Barry stood suddenly, his back as stiff as a board and rummaged for his wallet. He took out a twenty and slammed it down on the bar.

"Keep the change, Jake!" he blurted. Then he turned on a heel and marched straight out. Distantly, he heard Soupie say something about free drinks for all. Passing through the lobby, he heard the fat man's laughter chasing after him and sprinted for the elevator.

Back at his room, Barry found Peter sound asleep on top of the covers and the TV on. As gently as he could, he pulled down the blanket and coaxed the sleeping boy between the sheets. Then he undressed quickly and got into his own bed, rolled himself into a tight ball.

Peter waited as long as he could for his dad to come back. He wasn't hooked on the movie, even though he'd missed it at the theater. What he'd really wanted was to watch with Dad, talk about gadgets, maybe laugh a little bit. He'd finally stopped watching the door and channel surfed for a while. When he came back to the movie channel, he'd lost all track of what was going on in the story.

He was angry.

How could his dad just go off and leave him like that? He realized grown-ups had to live their own lives, but it was just as important for them to do what they said as it was for Peter. If Peter had gone off and been late coming back, Dad would have had hotel security combing the building for him. He could imagine having Dad paged in the lobby. That would piss him off for sure.

When he heard the door opening he got a quick idea. Pretend to be asleep. He shut his eyes and relaxed his grip on the remote. As he heard his dad's footsteps approaching, he caught the stink of cigarette smoke and liquor. Shit! He knew his dad wasn't supposed to be drinking booze, and he'd quit smoking as a promise to Peter three years ago.

"Peter," his dad whispered. Not loud enough to wake me up, Peter decided. He kept his eyes closed, relaxed his breathing as much as he could. To his surprise, his dad didn't try any harder to wake him up. *Damn* - Peter thought, *I'm going to have to go through with this.*

He felt his father's hands gently moving him on the bed, heard the covers being pulled down. His shoes came off, one at time. The next thing he knew, he was tucked in like a baby and it felt surprizingly good. He heaved a deep sigh and snuggled his cheek into the pillow. After a few moments, his eyelids got dark as his dad turned off the light and he heard the click of the TV shutting down. He opened his eyes and he was facing his father's bed. Under his covers, Dad had his legs pulled up, his body rolled into a tight ball.

A little surprised, Peter wondered if his dad always went to sleep that way.

Chapter 8

Morning came early, Barry saw as he compared the digital clock radio to his wristwatch. *Two time zones ahead* - he thought.

He rubbed his eyes, scratched his scalp and looked over at the boy. Still sleeping. Quietly, he rolled out of bed.

He peered out the blinds, letting a crack of bright sunshine into the room. It looked hot already. He went over to the suitcase which was still packed on a rack in the closet. He unzipped it and brought out his toilet bag; razor, small can of shaving gel, toothbrush and travel tube of baking soda toothpaste for tartar control. As he turned to go into the bathroom, he saw Peter leaning on one elbow looking at him.

"Ready for a ball game today?" Barry inquired.

Peter flopped back down and covered his head with his pillow, groaning.

Barry went in, closed the bathroom door behind him and took a leak. Then he opened the door six inches and began brushing his teeth. Over the sound of the water running, he heard heavy footsteps.

"Out! Get out!" Peter called as he trotted in the door. "I gotta go!"

Barry made a hasty exit, felt the door hit him in the ass as Peter closed it. He stood in front of the dresser mirror watching himself and continued brushing. Through the door, he heard a torrent of water.

At least he pees like a man - Barry thought with pride.

Peter didn't want to face his dad this morning. It had taken him over an hour to get to sleep the night before and he felt grouchy. At least he hadn't wakened up with a boner. That would have been embarassment beyond belief.

He flushed the commode and tried to avoid looking at himself in the mirror. He stared into the bathtub instead. Pretty soon, his dad knocked on the door.

"Mff, mff, mm, mm" Dad mumbled.

"Huh?" Peter hollered.

"MFF, MFF, MM, MM" Dad mumbled a little louder.

Finally, Peter opened the door and looked at his dad. "What did you say?"

Dad rushed over to the sink and spit.

"I said, can I come in. I have to rinse my mouth, for heaven sake."

"Well, why didn't you just say so?" Peter grinned into the mirror and met his dad's eyes. Dad was gargling and tried to say something deep in his throat. Then he spat out the water and rubbed the back of his hand across his lips.

"Very funny." He reached for the towel Peter handed him.

"Don't mention it." Peter padded into the other room and switched on the TV. Then he did a swan dive into the bed and bounced around awhile, enjoying his small victory over his father.

By the time Barry finished shaving his sideburns, cheeks, and neck, he was already hungry. The sound of TV cartoons kept him distracted from any other coherent thought.

"Hey, I want you to get dressed so we can go down to the restaurant for breakfast."

"Let's just get room service again."

"We did that last night. I want fresh coffee and lots of it, so get your butt in gear."

"Aw, Dad, do I have to?"

Barry stuck his head through the door and saw his son grinning like a Cheshire cat. He was already dressed and sitting on the edge of the bed, ready to go.

"Gotcha!"

"Well, just give me a few minutes to put on some fresh clothes and we can go. Meanwhile, don't you think you oughta brush your teeth at least?"

"Just waiting for you to get done, Pop."

A few minutes later, they were ready to head for the elevator, when Barry pulled himself up short.

"You know, Peter. It's been thirty-five years since I've been to Wrigley Field."

"You know, Pop. I've never been at all."

"This is going to be great!"

By the time they had breakfast, drove into the city, negotiated the Loop, found a parking place, and walked up Waveland Avenue to the ball park, the sun was directly overhead. Barry rolled up his sleeves and wiped his hands on his blue jeans.

The big difference was sweat.

In California, it got hot, but it was usually so dry that the moisture evaporated right away, cooling you off. In Chicago, the humidity was in the high seventies and hung there like a wet towel on a clothes line. You could reach out and touch it.

Barry was nonplussed that nobody else in the ticket lines seemed to mind, although there were dark crescents under every armpit. Their wait in the queue was rewarded with two seats in the second deck, down the left field line, ten rows back on an aisle. He knew they were lucky to get seats at all, since the Cubs were in a race for the National League Wild Card spot, and Sammy Sosa was in a duel with Mark McGuire for the home run crown.

They walked through the grandstands, among deep shadows and giant girders, smelling popcorn, peanuts, mustard, and beer. They hadn't gone fifty feet before Peter asked him for a pretzel and a Coke.

"Didn't you just eat breakfast?"

"That was an hour ago."

"OK, OK. Here's twenty bucks. Have at it."

Peter walked over to stand in line and Barry stood in an archway overlooking the left field bleachers and the outfield. Although it was still an hour to game time, the stands were full, at least in left. The grass was a thick carpet of green with darker green in the ivy growing up the bricks, separated by the reddish brown dirt of the warning track. On the field, the Cubs were taking their warm ups, running sprints, stretching out, and playing catch. He heard the crack of a bat and looked towards home plate.

A cage had been rolled out around home for batting practice and a pitcher stood on a mat in front of the mound lobbing change ups. There was another crack and he saw a long fly ball, the white, white baseball against the blue, blue sky, arch over the fence. The crowd cheered, including groups of fans on rooftops across the street. He couldn't tell who was up, but it was a dark, right hander and he bet it was Sosa. Another pitch and a line drive thunked the red brick behind the ivy in left. Barry's heart pounded.

He turned around to see Peter walking up with a pretzel in each fist and Cokes pressed against his ribs with his forearms.

"Hey, Dad. Little help here!"

Barry grabbed a cup and a pretzel, then looked beyond Peter, into the shadows. He did a double take as he saw Soupie, from the bar last night. She was arm in arm with the fat man, standing knee deep in the beer line. He tried to look away, but before he could, she noticed him and waved, sent him a wide grin. Next she blew him a kiss, then tried to get the fat man's attention. Quickly, Barry ducked through the archway.

"Hey, Dad. Where ya going?" Peter called behind him. But before he could get halfway down the grandstand, he heard the fat man's laugh and didn't wait for Peter to catch up. He stopped at the railing overhanging the field level seats, with nowhere to go except across the outstretched legs of fans on both sides of the aisle.

In a minute, Peter stood next to him with a bewildered look and mustard from his pretzel on his face.

"Hey, Pop, this isn't our section," Peter said.

"I know, I just wanted to see Sosa take batting practice."

A guy in the row back from the railing called out to Barry. "Yeah, buddy, we all want to see Sosa hit. How 'bout you find a seat?"

He apologized to the man and took the steep steps back up. When they were back in the darkness, he looked around but didn't see Soupie. Relieved, he made a show of checking their ticket stubs again and searching out the way. By the time they got to their seats, batting practice was over.

"Well, here we are," Barry said. The sun broiled them from overhead. Sweat trickled down his neck and under his shirt. He looked at Peter, laboring with the heat in the seat next to him.

"What time does the game start?" Peter asked.

"We've got about another half hour. It's twelve-thirty now."

"I wish I'd brought a hat."

"Me, too."

They sat in silence for a few moments until it dawned on Barry. This was the perfect time to hit the souvenir stands.

Thirty minutes later, Peter and his dad returned to their seats with an awkward, Cubs-blue plastic bag full of paraphenalia and memorabilia. There was a two-foot long blue bat, a Cubs pennant on a stick, a Wrigley Field coffee mug, a program with a pen shaped like a bat, several baseball cards mounted on wooden plaques, a large blue and red hand that pointed out "We're # 1!", a cuddly Cub Teddy bear for Martha, and an autographed baseball from Ernie Banks. The ball from Banks was an extravagance for Dad, who reasoned he wouldn't be around Chicago very often. They both wore new Cubs hats, which were the only practical things they bought.

"Jeez, Pop, why did we have to get so much stuff?" Peter complained. "All I wanted was a hat."

"Your mom always likes to pick up souvenirs for people, and you know how much she likes Teddy bears."

"Yeah, but she's an Astros fan. She hates the Cubs. Next time you get her a teddy, get her one she can wear to bed. And don't you think sixty-five dollars is a little too much to pay for a baseball?"

His dad looked at him incredulously.

"How do you know about what women wear to bed, young man? And besides, Ernie Banks is my favorite player. He's a Hall-of-Famer. Most home runs ever by a shortstop."

"Yeah, I know, and he's O. J. Simpson's uncle, too, but it's still too much money. Now if we could get one autographed by Sammy Sosa himself, that might be worth something."

"We could go down after the game and try if you like," Dad offered.

"Nah. It's going to be a mob scene. The game is gonna be a sell out."

Peter looked around him. Chicago fans had turned out in force. There were four guys a few sections down who had taken off their shirts. Their chests were painted with huge blue and red letters, and together they spelled CUBS.

The announcer invited everyone to stand for the National Anthem. Peter grudgingly took off his new Cubs cap already stained dark with sweat, and faced the scoreboard in center field. Hopefully, it would only be nine innings, but Peter knew it was going to be a long day.

He tugged his dad's arm. "Who the heck are we even playing, anyway?"

By the top of the seventh inning, Barry was more than ready to leave. He had spotted Soupie and the fat man in the crowd, several hundred feet away and had tried to remain inconspicuous. Then came the seventh.

The score was tied at 1-1. Sosa had homered in the second inning on a fastball low and in, a solo shot onto Waveland Avenue, but the opposing pitcher had settled into a groove and the bases had been empty since. The Cubs pitcher worked hard to keep pace, giving up three hits in the fourth that scored a run, but he stopped the bleeding with a high pop out, a home run in a telephone booth. In the seventh, after getting the leadoff man to ground out to short, he loaded the bases on two singles and a walk.

Barry sweated through the seat of his jeans and felt a heat rash coming on. To make it worse, the piching coach was out on the mound trying to settle his hurler down. After what seemed an eternity, he decided to leave him in.

The opposition was at the heart of the order, three men on, when the pitcher hung a breaking ball on the inside part of the plate to the clean up hitter. The crack of the bat followed the ball up into the steamy Chicago air and the crowd held its collective breath. The ball was well-hit, high and long, but hooking foul. Barry watched the arching curve streak across the sky. The crowd around him rose to their feet as one and suddenly Peter was standing up on the arms of his chair. The ball came closer, starting to lose momentum until it bounced into a gaggle of upraised arms in the rows ahead of them. Barry watched Peter, afraid that he might slip and fall, but Peter was intent on the ball. Suddenly, it popped up and out of the crowd of hands and carommed straight to Peter. He caught it with both hands, then held the ball up to the loud cheers of the people around. Barry could not hear his own voice, but he knew he was cheering as loud as he could, too. Then the crowd settled down again, like the surface of the sea when oil is poured over it.

Back on the field, the pitcher wound and delivered, a low fastball that the batter drove down on and one-hopped to the third baseman. It was a bang bang 5-4-3 double play and the Cubs were out of the inning. It all happened so fast, Barry didn't know whether to look at the field or his son, but found himself holding on to both of his shoulders and shaking him with happiness.

"Whoo, I got it!"

"Hey, hey, hey, you got it!"

All the fans around them pounded Peter on the back. "Way to go, kid!" "Nice catch!" "Aw right, Cubbies!"

Next thing he knew, Barry turned around to the aisle and she grabbed him, threw her arms around his neck and pressed her face up against his. Her mouth found his and he felt her tongue pry between his lips with the taste of beer and lipstick on it. Her firm breasts pushed him in the chest and he nearly fell over. Above it all, he heard the laugh of the fat man standing behind her on the steps.

Horror filled him, but *damn* she was a good kisser!

Before he knew it, she had placed Peter's face between her hands and she was giving him a big kiss on the mouth.

"Jesus, that's my kid!" he shouted.

The fat man grabbed him by the shoulder and spun him around. Breath of onions and beer engulfed him.

"Hey, whatsa matter?" the fat man rumbled. "The kid made a good catch. Let him get a little reward. Ha ha ha ha ha." His laugh rolled over Barry like a wave.

Suddenly, a sharp pain pounded his arm at the shoulder and Soupie had hit him right on his bruise.

"So where'd you go last night?" Soupie asked. "You left the party early."

Barry was really steamed now. "Look, I got a kid to take care of. We're trying to watch a ball game. I don't know what you think you're doing, but I don't appreciate . . . " He felt the fat man grab his sleeve.

"Easy, buddy. I don't want you should hurt the lady's feelings," Fat Man said.

"Aw, he's no fun," she said with a pout.

"Down in front," somebody shouted. The game had resumed, with the Cubs coming to bat.

"Dad, who are these people?" Peter asked, wiping at a smear of lipstick Soupie had left on his mouth.

"Come on, son. We gotta go." He grabbed Peter's hand and pushed past Fat Man on the stairs.

"But Dad," Peter protested, "the game's still tied."

"To hell with the game. We're getting outta here."

As he reached the cool shadow of the overhang and the concession area, he heard the sound of a woman's laughter chasing him, a sound like bells. It echoed in his ears all the way to their rental car on Waveland Avenue.

Chapter 9

The car tilted over at a wicked angle and Peter was surprised they didn't skid. Dad took corners faster than usual, and this was a strange car. That couldn't be good. He still had no idea what had happened.

"Take it easy, Dad. You're gonna get a ticket."

"It's OK. Everythings fine. Can you find the buttons for the air-conditioning? And maybe get us a radio station."

"The radio's on your station already. Can't you hear the ball game? The Cubs just scored three runs on a homer."

"What?" his dad asked and looked at him with wild eyes. There was red lipstick from the lady all over his mouth and sweat had beaded and dried on his forehead. The air-conditioning was already blasting.

"Easy does it!" They narrowly missed colliding with a bus making a right hand turn ahead of them. They followed the bus around the corner and turned south. Peter saw a sign that read "Lakeshore Drive". His dad merged left and stepped hard on the gas, then hit the brakes as traffic came to a standstill in front of them.

"Jesus!" Peter said. "Why don't we pull over someplace and get a Coke? There's a McDonald's up ahead and I could sure use one." Dad didn't answer.

Five minutes later, they'd driven the two blocks to the drive-thru restaurant and pulled into the parking lot. Traffic was a zoo, but they had the city skyline to their left. Across the wide boulevard, Lake Michigan stretched out before them, white caps and white clouds to the horizon. Peter kept quiet, enjoying the stillness. A stiff breeze off the lake rocked the car gently.

"I'm sorry."

Peter said nothing.

"I said I'm sorry."

Peter just shrugged.

On the radio, the game came back from commercial and they listened to the top of the ninth inning. Rod Beck closed out the opponents for his fortieth save of the year, striking out two batters. Peter was sorry he hadn't got the chance to see the big guy pitch.

"It's OK, Dad," he finally said, after the announcer had cut to commercial again. Peter switched off the radio. "But why did that lady kiss me?"

"I have no idea. I met her last night at the motel and she was just as strange then."

"You actually know this person?"

"I mean we met at the bar and had a conversation. I don't know her from Adam and Eve. And as far as I'm concerned, she's crazy."

"Crazy is right," Peter said. "I thought she was trying to grab my baseball." He held up the ball and showed it to his dad. The black lettering *Official Ball* and "National League" stood out.

Then Dad's face turned ugly. "Shit," he said.

"What's the matter?" Peter's blood turned icy.

"Our stuff. We left all our stuff at the ball park. That was almost two hundred dollars worth of junk . . . My Ernie Banks autographed baseball."

Anguish flooded Peter and his face burned. They were miles away now. There was no way they could get back to the ball park to look for their bag.

"I'm sorry," Peter mumbled under his breath and suddenly his dad seemed in better spirits. He reached for his Coke and Peter flinched, thinking it was an act, that he might lash out with his hand or fist even, but he actually seemed to be feeling better.

"That's OK," Dad said, sipping his drink. "We didn't need all that junk anyway. The way I see it, we made a clean getaway."

"Yeah. A clean getaway." Peter didn't really agree, but he was willing to go along.

"There's another game tomorrow, same time, same place, if you're willing to suffer through the heat again."

"I could do that." He wanted to shout *Boy, would I!*, but knew that would be too demonstrative. Secretly, that's about all he wanted right now, to see a whole game, maybe even catch another foul ball. He was more grateful to his dad than he wanted to let on for understanding things for a change.

Dad pointed across the street. "You see that building over there? The one with the big white dome? That's the Museum of Science and Industry. Did you know they have a real World War II submarine in there."

"No," Peter said, disbelievingly. "A whole submarine?"

Afternoon at the museum led to dinner in a downtown bar and grill. His dad swore by the steaks and Peter had to admit they were pretty good. Charcoal broiled, they tasted just like the one's Dad cooked at home, black on the outside and juicy pink inside. He was especially glad when his father ordered non-alcoholic beer and let Peter take a swig. The malty taste reminded him of summer at the beach, coming home thirsty enough to drink salt water.

After ice cream, they decided to take in a movie. Peter had wanted to see the new blockbuster, Armaggeddon, and they found it in a movie section from the paper. They walked the few blocks to the theater, looking up at the deep blue evening sky between the tall buildings. It was like hiking down a canyon made out of skyscrapers. Dad pointed out the Prudential Building, its top stories aflame with orange sunset, reflecting the high clouds. The afternoon had been completely clear, but puffy clouds were sailing in off the lake. They were gunmetal gray on one edge, and pink like the steaks on the other.

The theater was in one of the tall buildings. Its lobby had huge chandaliers, like the ones Peter had seen back home at Symphony Hall. But he wasn't used to seeing them in a movie theater. The seats were deep and plush, a red velvet curtain across the screen before the previews. Armaggeddon was as expected, lots of fireworks display special effects, huge comets slamming into the earth. But the part Peter liked the best was the relationship between the hero and his daughter. She didn't know if she'd ever see her father again, or her husband, for that matter, but dads always come through in the end. Especially in the movies.

Peter slept on the way home in the car, listening to soft, classical music. Dad hadn't felt like talking and so he just dropped off. It was peaceful, the rocking of the car, the singing of the tires on the expressway.

When Barry returned to the Holiday Inn, he asked for any messages at the front desk. He'd tried to call Martha from the restaurant pay phone, but the machine had picked up, so he expected she might try to call. But to his surprise and chagrin, the only message consisted of a note attached to a big blue plastic bag. Inside were all the things he'd left behind at Wrigley Field. The note was simple, on motel paper.

Sorry you left in such a hurry. It's not what you think. If you want to talk about it, come by room 222.
Sophie

He took the bag, then crumpled up the note and put it in the trash.

Peter felt ecstatic that their stuff was waiting for them at the front desk. He saw his dad toss a crumpled bit of paper into the trash can by the elevator and wondered who it was from. Then he knew.

"It's from the lady, isn't it, Dad?" He was still dopey from his nap in the car, so his voice sounded more excited than he wanted it to.

The elevator opened, but Dad didn't answer.

Wow - Peter thought, *what a stroke of luck. Maybe she wasn't so crazy after all.*

He listened to the Musak coming out of the ceiling as they rode the elevator car to the third floor. He could see their blurry reflections in the metal door, his dad only half a head taller than him anymore. He felt like he'd grown six inches in one day. Then he knew what he had to do.

"Hey, Pop," he said. "I know it's late, but I was wondering if it would be OK, just for a little while, can I go swimming?"

To his surprise, his dad cracked a grin.

"Hey, it's after ten, but what the heck. I'll go with you."

Oily cool fingers caressed his face, a stream of air rushing out of his nose as he swam towards the milky white light underwater. He could see his hands stretched out, with hundreds of tiny silver bubbles, like a skin of shiny froth, covering his arms. There, by the light, Peter treaded water. Then Barry came up for air.

"That's two," he said, taking in a huge gasp of air to fill his aching lungs. "Two times across. Top that, squid."

Peter wore a broad grin, his eyes sparkling. "Just watch," he said. He took a gulp of air and slid under, pushing off powerfully with his legs.

Barry watched his son zoom away like a torpedo. "Fire one," he said under his breath, proud to see the boy becoming such a capable swimmer. The night was empty, with no other swimmers and the hum of the giacuzzi pump the only sound at pool side. Clorine pinched his nose and stung his eyes, but the water felt like silk on his skin.

If only Martha were here, we could slip into silk kimonos and snuggle in the pillows . . .

His fantasy was interrupted by Peter breaking water like a whale next to him. They laughed. Then Peter spotted something over Barry's shoulder.

"Hey, Dad, lookit that."

Barry looked and saw, at the edge of the circle of lights around the pool area, the glowing red eyes of an animal. He looked closer and saw that it was a skinny, long-haired dog, sniffing at the pool air. Peter called to him.

"Hey, don't get him over here. He's probably just some stray."

But the dog walked over as if he owned the place, came right up to Barry and kissed him on the cheek with his nose, then went to Peter and licked him vigorously on the face, to Peter's obvious delight. Barry could see the dog had a variety of markings, from collie to shepherd to golden retriever, a big dog with a long snout and pointed ears, but definitely a unique sort of mut. Barry didn't have the heart to shoo him away.

Then as quick as he had come, the dog departed, scampering into the night.

They laughed some more and dunked each other under the water, splashing and making an uproarious ruckous. Then Barry upended and dived for the bottom. He would see how long he could stay under water. Up above him, he could see Peter peek down into the water, then make spashing sounds like depth charges dropped from an enemy destroyer. He felt he could hold his breath for ever, maybe just as easily take a breath of water and breath normally. He had half a mind to try it.

From the surface, there came a huge splash as a body knifed into the water. It came straight to Barry and he had no choice but to fend off the hands that took him by the armpits and turned him around. Before he knew what had happened, he was on top of the water and face to face with Soupie, her black hair slicked back like a seal and her eyes blinking away water. Then she dove down and resurfaced behind him, got him in a cross-chest carry and swam with him to the side of the pool. He'd been so startled he couldn't move, but at poolside he regained his powers of motion and speech.

"Soupie, what the hell do you think you're doing?"

"I'm saving your life, saving your life." She was out of breath.

"For God's, woman. Are you crazy?" Barry hoisted himself onto the patio, water streaming off his body.

"Wait," she said. "Wait, it's time for mouth to mouth resuccitation."

Barry was amazed that she knew the word, let alone could pronounce it, so he stopped and walked back to the edge of the pool. Looking down at Soupie, he could see she was wearing an evening dress of sorts, her bosoms floating free in the limpid pool water, lovely and suprizingly inviting. She saw him notice and tried to find her broken straps and cover up.

"Somebody needs to resuccitate your brain," he said. Then he noticed Peter, still in the pool and trying to stifle his shock and laughter.

"What are you laughing at?"

"'Resuccitate your brain.' Duh, good one, Pop," Peter aped.

Then he saw how ridiculous the whole scene was and offered a hand to his drenched, would-be saviour.

"Come on. Alley oop," he said.

She emerged with her clothes dripping off of her, bare feet gripping the deck through drenched hose.

"Oh, shit," she said. "My shoes are down there somewhere."

"Oh, brother." Barry dived down to the bottom and retrieved her black pumps, which no doubt were ruined anyway. He surfaced again and swam to the side, presenting the heels to Soupie. He couldn't help notice how her soaked clothing made the curves of her hips and buttocks stand out, powerfully erotic.

Prototypically feminine - Barry thought. Then it hit him - *That's how I saw Martha - when she was pregnant.*

"Well, I guess you were ready again," he said as he exited the water and sat on the tiled side.

"Yup, that's me. Ready, willing and able to make a complete fool of myself."

"Ahem." Peter treaded water next to Barry. "Don't you think it's time to introduce your son?"

Barry introduced them, matter-of-factly, no fanfare, went over and fetched a towel to wrap around her shoulders.

"Thank you," she said.

"I suppose it's time to thank *you*, if not for saving my life, for the thought, at least. And thank you for bringing our things from the ball park. I'm sorry I had to leave in such a hurry."

"Well, I guess you're welcome on both counts, but I really have to go now. Change clothes, whatever, rescue my lost self-esteem . . . Peter, it was nice to meet you and congratulations on catching that ball. Now I gotta go. Oh God." Her voice showed how distraught she was and she ran away towards the motel, entered the side door and disappeared.

Peter and Barry exchanged a look that embodied their common thought.

She's crazy.

Barry tossled Peter's hair as they walked back towards their hotel room in the hot night air. Since he was wet anyway, he hardly noticed the humidity, although he didn't seem to be drying off at all, dripping on the sidewalk in footsteps that became puddles.

"What's up with that lady, Dad? Why's she keep following us around?"

"Beats me. Maybe she was watching us out the window and thought I stayed down too long."

"Or maybe that was her dog, and she was out taking him for a walk."

"Nothing about that woman would surprise me." They entered the building and Barry pushed the button for the elevator. The door opened right away. "But let's go back to the room and forget about her. It's been a long day and I want to go to church tomorrow."

"Aw, church. Do I have to?"

"It's the church I grew up in, so I really want to go. I would appreciate it if you go with me."

Peter hung his head and Barry almost relented and told him he didn't have to go. But then he looked up and seemed OK with it.

"So it's settled," Barry said. He felt good, like he was able to put unpleasant things behind him somehow, things that would have led to arguments back home. When he pushed too hard to get his way, he inevitably ran into deep trouble, but today he sensed he was going to be all right, like some kind of faith was propelling him on his way. He'd felt it earlier, in the city, when he discovered he'd left their bag of souvenirs at the ball park. And that had turned out OK. Now, with the incident at the pool behind them, and the potential conflict over church resolved, he breathed in a fresh breath of well-being. *Thank God for small victories* - he thought.

They reached the room and took turns showering off the chlorine from the pool, with Barry going first. While Peter was in the bathroom, he decided to try the telephone again. Surely Martha would be home by now. It must be after ten o'clock in California.

The phone rang twice and she picked up.

"It's me," he said. They exchanged affections, caught up on the day. Then Martha explained her absence.

"Anne from the church called and invited me to dinner. I had nothing planned so I said fine. She is such a nice woman. Knows this great little restaurant down in the Gas Lamp Quarter. I'll have to take you there sometime."

Barry related how dinner with Peter had gone, then Martha went back to the subject of Anne.

"She's concerned about you, in a confident sort of way. Says it sounds like you're on what she called a journey to wholeness, sort of a pilgrimage. Talking to her made me feel better about the whole thing."

"Well, I'm glad for that anyway. But I haven't even thought about those dreams the whole time we've been here. I'm just having a good time with Peter, trying to get reconnected."

"Reconnected?" Martha drawled. "You make it sound like one of your power grids back in electric land."

"Coming on this trip seems to have really thrown the switch."

"Maybe when you get back you could connect me up, Mister Electrician."

"I'll put on the old tool belt if you like."

"Only if you let me talk you into taking it off again."

About that time Peter came out of the bathroom, a towel wrapped around his waist and another over his head.

"Say hi to Peter. He's turned into a regular fish. Swam across the pool twice underwater. You should have seen it. Here you go."

He handed the receiver to Peter, then went over to the window and looked out across the courtyard. He checked that the pool was empty, then circled the grounds with his eyes, half expecting to see Soupie, or perhaps the strange dog, prowling in the bushes.

Peter said good by to Martha and held the phone out to Barry. "She wants to say good night to you," he said.

He walked back to the beds and put the phone to his ear.

"What's this I hear about you and a strange lady meeting up all day long?"

Barry's blood turned to Coca Cola, and his heart skipped. "It really was nothing. Just some strange woman who kept showing up unexpectedly."

"Unexpectedly is right."

"Look, don't worry about it. I'm not. I'm sure it won't happen again and that's the last we'll see of her. You can ask Peter yourself when we get home."

"Well, I know you, so I'm not gonna worry one bit. Just don't forget we have a date when you get home."

"It's a date then."

"Oh, and Barry . . . Anne said to remind you to do your homework. She said you'd know what that means, OK?"

"Right. I know. Thanks, Honey."

They said good bye and Barry pushed down the switchhook on the base of the phone.

Homework - he thought, *but there's something I've got to do first.*

Quickly, before he changed his mind, he dialed 222.

She picked up halfway through the first ring.

Barry felt ready to vent, but her soft hello on the phone took the edge off his anger.

"Look," he began, "I know we keep running into each other, but I'm a married man and I'm really not interested in any further contact. Is that clear?"

"Yes, perfectly, but can't you give me thirty seconds to explain so you won't think I'm the crazy person you already think I am."

"All right. Thirty seconds. Starting now."

"OK, I just broke up with my husband we live in West Chicago and I came to see my cousin Don because he's the only person I can really talk to and the fat guy was nice enough to let me sleep on his couch and then had an extra ticket for the game so I said what the hell and he had to fly back to Olympia, Washington, but he let me keep his motel room one more night 'cause I didn't want to go home and face the music. OK, you got all that?"

"Huh? Listen, I'm sorry if I led you on in any way, because that was never my intent."

"Look, Barry, you seem like a nice guy and I just thought maybe we had a little something going on, but I was wrong. Besides I was too drunk last night to make new friends anyway, you know what I mean?"

"No hard feelings, then. In another life, it might have been possible."

"Just possible, huh? I thought I had you dead on."

"We both thought wrong. I gotta go. It's been nice knowing you, OK?"

"There's still time for you to change your mind."

"Good-bye, Soupie," he said firmly, then hung up the phone.

Barry stared at the phone a moment, then looked at his son grinning at him.

"What the heck kind of name is Soupie, anyway?" Peter asked.

"Don't say a word. I'm going to sleep."

Chapter 10

Towers of the dark castle rose like storm clouds, stark and perilous above wind-swept waves that crashed against stone ramparts. Below a jagged ridge of cliffs, a single dirt track ran, etched into the stone face. The path began at the mouth of a cave, barely tall enough for the man to emerge erect, the gloom behind him falling away into deep caverns. In the dream, Barry became the man, dressed in leather and iron, a warrior's battle garb. He looked down at his arms, sinewy and bulging with muscles clenched, a sword in one hand, a shield in the other.

The sea became calm, smoothed by a strong breath of wind that blew from the land towards the horizon, ruffling the tops of waves which glinted golden with the last vestiges of sunlight. The castle fell away to become a city, tall buildings topped by gunmetal gray clouds tinged with pink. The cliffs dissolved into a stone jetty which jutted into the waves, piled high with dancing froth. Barry looked at his arms but they had become long and smooth, the arms of a woman, his own body becoming a graceful curve against the wind, gossamer garments flowing around him. The womanly center of his being yearned for the sea, for the salt and brine, to become part of it, an aching need that made him want to leap into the arms of the waves.

Part of him held back and he became a dancer, a man leaping across a floor, landing and spinning on one foot. The dance was ballet, and he held his arms out to receive the form of a woman pirouetting towards him. Then he became the woman, enraptured in arching flight, which, to his surprise, turned to sorrow as he leaned down at the wet floor in a vast bath chamber, picked up a white towel and began to dry his naked body. His skin was rough, like sandpaper and he saw that his hands had turned black, that his entire body was black and he opened his mouth to scream. The sound that came out was singing, a primitive chant that blended into a jazz scat, in which he held long notes with impeccable inflection.

He was himself again in a museum for a brief instant, in a room full of strangers which he began to walk through, each of them absorbed in some activity or emotion. As he strode through the huge, vaulted room, to his stark terror, he became each of the strangers one at a time. With each step, he become another person, an athlete, a young woman, a rock and roll guitarist, a soldier, a priest, another dancer, actors and dancers in succession and he realized he was performing some kind of drama, a frightening story that changed scenes and purpose with each moment, flashing from one movie into another, interspersed, over and over. As soon as he became aware of one feeling in each position, he changed to the next, never able to hold any particular set of changes, or become himself again, which he willed himself to do. If I can just become myself, he reasoned on a calm level that seemed detached from what he was experiencing, I can stop the cycle, I can resolve the predicament. The harder he willed himself forward, the faster the changes became. Then with a great effort of will, he lunged forward and for an instant felt that he had become himself. That instant expanded to stillness all around him as he became frozen in the dream.

Instead of becoming others, he became himself, but younger, at each phase a different and younger version of himself, superimposed on each other. Younger and younger and on the edges of the dream feelings spinning in a kaleidoscope of color, a cyclone of hues careening around him, beginning with deep blue and progressing through green and then violet, and the younger he got the more red edged his image. Red became pain as he became younger until he realized all was taking place during one breath, one great exhale. He was a child, then a toddler, then an infant, until he came to rest on his back, devoid of all breath, intense pain surrounding him.

Red pain gave way to white light. A floating sensation filled him, ecstatic well-being. He was suffused with light, gentle and warm, uplifting and buoyant. Time extended to nothingness all around him, as if tippling in a universe of uniform white plasma, swimming in a bottle of milk he thought to himself, and then plunged into the dream again. He was in a room full of people, all actors talking to one another, as if celebrating some great accomplishment. He wandered among the groups of others, none of whom seemed to notice him, which was fine with him. He had a drink in his hand and he tasted it, realized it was champagne. Then he felt himself begin to change again, change into another person and fear gripped him. He willed himself not to change and in that instant he woke up.

The room was pitch dark, the hum of the air-conditioner steady and calming. He sat up and arranged the pillows behind his back, thought about the dream. He felt emotions swirling around inside of him, as if all the feelings of his being were set in motion, not in tumult or agitated, but active, alive. He breathed deeply and held still, wondering if the sensation of changing in the dream was still with him. It was not. As he looked inside, he sensed the same feelings, a vast variety of possibilities, none of which presented themselves in particular at the moment. Detached, he exhaled his breath, let himself breath easy.

Wow - he thought to himself. *That was the farthest out dream yet!*

He looked at his watch and realized it was four thirty in the morning, but he wasn't tired at all. He felt excited and energized. He remembered the message from Anne to do his homework. He realized he was now two dreams behind. His fever dream had been left in the lurch. The Wizard of Oz dream, a dream that had united his past with his present, had somehow catapulted him into an unforeseen future that became more frighteningly real than anything he could ever have imagined.

There's no time like the present - he thought, fearing that uncertain future.

He decided to get to work writing and he clicked on the reading lamp to find paper and a pen. He had to get up and walk over to the writing desk and when he did he opened the blinds to let in a little more light. He glanced outside, saw the hotel security lights, then returned to the cone of illumination at his bed. Everything in the room seemed to glow with an electric luminosity and he wondered if he was having an acid flashback. He sat back, relaxed, realized he was calm, that his mind was clear, as lucid as he had ever felt. He began to write:

Woke up early, before dawn, from the farthest out dream yet. Like every LSD trip rolled into one, a brilliant new movie, hip and sexy, full of amazing technology. Miraculous . . .

Barry worked on his new journal until he ran out of hotel stationary, then saw it was getting light outside, dark clouds with a tinge of red in the east. He noticed with satisfaction that the calm feeling from the white light, what seemed to be the center of the dream experience, had stayed with him.

There's that euphoria again - he told himself, *But what's false about it? I'm still alive and where there's life, there's hope. Anne told me that.*

He went to the bathroom and took his morning dose of Prozac, twenty milligrams. Then, pleased with his efforts to assimilate what his dream had showed him, he dressed quietly and went out to find a cup of coffee.

Chapter 11

Peter had to admit, it felt good to sleep in.

When he awoke, Dad was nowhere to be seen. He called out to see if he was in the bathroom, but the only sound was the hum of the air-conditioner. No matter. He wasn't anxious to go to church anyway. Checking the clock radio on the night table, he saw it was only eight-thirty, barely an indulgence at all, but he felt luxuriously rested. He decided not to bother with the television. A quiet room for once seemed enough.

After dozing a few more minutes, he got up, leisurely pulled on a pair of shorts, went to the bathroom and did his thing, brushed his wavy brown hair and checked out his face. *What happened to that pimple from the other night? Barely noticeable. Hey, is that a whisker on my chin. Nah. Just a smudge of dirt.* He decided to wash thoroughly, hot water, soap, washcloth, the whole bit.

Now he felt ready, but where was Dad?

He put on his sandals and a clean shirt and headed down to check the restaurant.

Dad was sitting at a table in a corner, half hidden by a large potted plant. Peter saw that he had already eaten breakfast, the remains set aside to make room for a huge Sunday paper. The front page read *Tribune.* But instead of reading the paper, it looked like Dad was writing a letter.

"Hey, Pop. Whatcha up to?"

"Not much. Have a seat, or you can get yourself some breakfast over there." Dad pointed to a buffet piled high with plates of fruit and muffins, hot pans steaming with what looked like hash brown potatoes, scrambled eggs, and pancakes.

"I smell bacon!" Peter fetched a plate and then, like a dog searching out a rabbit, visited each hot spot and filled his dish in a matter of seconds. *Well* - he reasoned, *I can always come back for more.*

Back at the table, he flopped down across from Dad just as the waiter in a white coat approached with the coffee pot.

"Oh, no, I'm full," his dad told the waiter, putting his palm on top of his cup.

"I'm not," Peter said. He shoved his own cup forward.

"Would you like cream with your coffee this morning, sir?" the waiter asked with a slight latino accent. The middle-aged man had dark skin and a pencil-thin mustache. His smile was friendly beneath deep, brown eyes.

"Yes, cream and sugar, please."

"Your sugar is right here," he said, scooting a small holder with a stack of sugar packets towards Peter from the edge of the table. "I'll be right back with your cream."

His dad didn't say a word, but his eyebrows arched as Peter took two sugars and shook them between his thumb and forefinger. He tore one edge off the small paper envelopes and dumped sugar in his cup, watching steam hover over the surface like morning mist on a small, black lake. A second later, the waiter wordlessly placed a small white pitcher near Peter's hand.

"Thank you, very much," his dad said, beating Peter to the punch.

"You're welcome. Would you like some orange juice? It's fresh squeezed."

"Yes, please," Peter said. The waiter left with a slight bow.

"Since when are you drinking coffee?" Dad asked appreciatively.

Peter didn't flinch, but inside he felt satisfied. His mother had showed him how to fix his coffee a few weeks before, but he had only had it twice. This was the third time. He added a splash of cream, the thick white liquid billowing like a cloud and turning the coffee a dark tan. He sniffed it.

"Mmmmm."

A glass pitcher of orange juice and two glasses appeared on their table from the waiter, who didn't pause for thanks.

"Would you like a section of the paper, perhaps the funnies?" Dad asked.

"Can't read now, eating." Peter knew the reference to Homer Simpson was lost on his dad. He jammed a forkfull of eggs in his mouth. They were hot and firm, just a hint of onion and spice. He suddenly longed for ketchup and looked around the table for the bottle. There was none and he looked farther for the nice waiter in the white coat. As he turned to glance over his shoulder, the man appeared, offered Peter a shiny bottle of catsup. He took it gratefully and twisted off the cap.

"Thank you very much," Peter mumbled around his eggs. He shook the bottle and to his amazement, a big blob of ketchup oozed out of the mouth of the bottle and dripped onto his eggs with no effort at all.

"Very good, sir," the waiter said, then hurried away, as if to prepare another bottle for someone else in dire need of tomato sauce.

Peter ate in silence, unconcerned for anything else in the world.

After a few minutes, his dad got up to leave.

"I'm going back to the room. Just sign the check and show the cashier your room key. Make sure you leave your friend the waiter a nice tip. Twenty percent, OK?"

"Mmmpff." Peter nodded his head in the affirmative.

"We leave for church in forty-five minutes."

D'oh! - Peter thought.

Chapter 12

Barry saw clouds building above the tree tops on the way to church. He remembered the way like it was yesterday. Trinity Episcopal was a red-brick box that was dwarfed by a six story steel and stained glass structure, what must have been one of the tallest buildings in town. The office building occupied a corner of two oak-lined streets a block north of the downtown area and two blocks west of the Old Library.

"The original Church was built in 1910," Barry said, "but they didn't tear it down after the new one. They stood side by side for years. Us kids had Sunday school and morning prayer in the old church as far back as I remember. Now I guess they've built those offices." He pointed towards the tall building on the corner. A trim garden fit between the two buildings, flanking the walkway to a Parish Hall the size of a small gymnasium.

Why did they have to change everything? - Barry wondered, knowing it was inevitable.

He pulled the car into a space in the lot behind the church and they walked around to the front. A small group of worshippers waited there before going in, a woman and two small children, and an elderly couple. The old woman smiled warmly at Barry, then went in the door, which the man held open for her.

The organ started playing and he recognized Bach, the opening strains of *Jesu, Joy of Man's Desiring*. Then the strangest thing: Peter was wearing a big smile.

Peter hadn't let Dad know how much he enjoyed coming to church, especially the music. *It doesn't fit my casual air of nonchallance* - he told himself, *and classical music was decidedly uncool. Besides, then I might have to go every Sunday and use up my whole weekend!*

He also liked watching the acolytes in their black and white robes, which made them look like angels carrying candles. There was a pair of boys, both younger than Peter, walking behind another tall boy in a red robe, a teenager with long hair like Jesus who carried the cross in front of the whole procession. Peter imagined himself doing that job.

Yeah -he thought, *I could handle it, no problem.*

The service got complicated, as usual, changing from hymn books to prayer books to specially printed pages, standing up, kneeling down, sitting, then waiting while the priest gave a sermon with jokes that Peter didn't get. All the same, he felt good about it. And he loved the singing. Of course, Dad knew all the moves and changes by heart. After more than an hour of singing and praying, they finally got around to a prayer that Peter knew. It began with *Our Father*, and from there he could follow right along. From that point, he felt caught up in the spirit of the thing, all the coming and going, fumbling with the wafer at the railing and getting a taste of real wine. He knew it was supposed to be blood, but there was no getting away from that smell. It was wine and he got a big gulp.

After the service, they waiting in line to shake the priest's hand. They didn't know anybody, of course. Serveral people introduced themselves, and were told how proud he was of his son, even though Peter felt uncomfortable as hell being introduced to strangers he'd never see again. Not only that, he felt underdressed in his T-shirt and shorts, even if they were clean. It was a small consolation that Dad was wearing a golf shirt instead of a tie.

Soon, they stood on the sidewalk, feeling the heat of the day build. He asked Dad the time and it was only eleven-thirty. Plenty of time to make Wrigley Field.

"Aw, Dad, do we have to go?"

"It will only take a few minutes, you'll see." His dad steered the car away from the expressway and turned down another tree-lined street. Peter was beginning to think all the streets in the town looked exactly alike, with postage stamp front yards and steps leading up from the sidewalk to front porches with swings on them. He certainly couldn't tell one kind of tree from another, but Dad kept pointing them out. That was an elm tree, that one a maple, that one over there was something called a box elder. He just knew he wanted to go to the baseball game and Dad was going to make them late.

They finally crossed a main street and turned into a neighborhood that looked a little bit different. The houses were run down instead of just being old. Not like the large two and three story homes that reminded him of the houses in movies like *Home Alone* and *Rookie of the Year*, these were all single floors, with many of them in real need of a paint job. The yards were mostly cut, but they had cars parked in some of them, cars that looked like they hadn't moved in years.

"Whoa," his Dad said. "It looks like the old neighborhood has gone downhill."

"You lived here?" The thought of his dad growing up in one of these crackerbox houses did not appeal to Peter.

"They sure seemed a lot bigger when I was a kid."

They cruised around a corner, drove down another street.

"There," his dad said. "That one with the awning over the front porch."

Peter looked at a two-tone house with a green canvas awning over the front door. A tall maple tree grew out of the front lawn and the grass thinned out inside the circle of shade underneath it.

"That's it, Pop?"

"Yup. 1955 Delano Road."

"Pop, it's a dump."

"Your grandfather had it built just for us. There were three bedrooms, living room, dining room, even a family room where he put up a whole paper mache village with an H & O railroad set. He spent hours working on that train."

"Maybe he should have spent some time working on the yard," Peter said.

Dad gave him a sad kind of look, and he knew he was dissappointed. "I was hoping it would be in better shape, maybe all fixed up nice."

Above the rooftop, Peter saw the dark clouds gathering, towering into the sky. It looked like it would start raining any minute.

"Are we going to make it to the game OK?" he asked.

Dad looked at his watch. "You know, I forgot all about it. It isn't even twelve o'clock yet. We've got plenty of time, depending on the traffic."

"Maybe we could get going?"

"Right!" His dad gunned the motor and put the car in gear. They leaped forward, the little rental car doing its best to get them there on time. "Those clouds are looking pretty ugly."

"We're not going to get rained out, are we, Dad?"

"Nah. We might get a delay, though. They won't let them play if there is thunder and lightning." He turned the corner and they motored through the last block of the neighborhood. "Say good-bye to the old homestead."

Peter saw the street sign at the corner by the stop sign. The four-lane highway was Roosevelt Road. The street they were on was Greenwood. They turned right and headed east, the general direction of Chicago. After another block, they approached a railroad crossing. To Peter's dismay, the lights were flashing and the crossarm was coming down.

"Hurry up, Dad!"

The car came to an abrupt stop as the striped barricade came down in front of them.

"Oh, man!" Peter said. He saw the dark clouds low above tops of the trees across the highway. It was like dusk, as though the sun had already set for the evening. "Oh, nuts," Peter said, "it's really going to rain." He looked at his dad for reassurance, but he was staring past Peter, his eyes locked in on something over his shoulder. Peter heard the horn from the train and turned to look.

Barry felt frozen, as if his sweat had turned to a thin sheet of ice all over his skin. In front of him, the barricade was a row of flashing red lights slung between the front of the car and their only escape route. It was as dark as night outside and he started to reach for the headlight switch. Then he saw the train.

It must have been a quarter of a mile to the south, approaching like a huge beast, the steel grill on the front of the locomotive gleaming even in the gloom. Behind the engine, a long line of box cars stretched out, as if pushing the train, urging it forward. He heard the horn blast.

Panic hit him and he suddenly knew. It was the fever dream, not the Wizard of Oz that had made him come back to visit his old home town. Not the white light and floating that made him feel like he had been born again. It was a warning. The train was coming and everything was about to fly apart. Then he saw Peter, his head turned to watch the train approach out the car window. Suddenly he knew what was about to happen, what the dream had warned him about for all these years. Disaster was about to strike, and Barry had led them right into it. He'd been warned but had not understood. Now it was too late. The train was almost upon them. They were about to die.

His arms would not move, other than to shake in the sockets of his shoulders. He wanted to reach for the gear lever, but his hands had turned to stone. His eyes glanced in the rearview mirror, saw the line of cars pulled up behind him. To his left, another car waited at the the crossing. Beyond the other car was a filling station with an ancient pump and Barry remembered the wreck of an old car that had been parked there for weeks when he was a kid, the front end smashed and crumpled like an accordian. The other drivers could not know. He was the only one who knew. He tried to speak but could only make something like a croak in his throat. Peter turned to look at him, eyes wide with excitement when they should be full of fear. In a second it would be over. The signal bell clanged in rythmn with his heart. His ears pounded with pressure.

The train was upon them. It roared like a tornado ten feet from the front of the car, rocking the chasis on its springs. Barry wanted to cry out, but felt like an iron hand had clamped his throat, strangling him. The rush of noise came like a blow, and then there was a steady roar and the clack of iron wheels on steel rails. Barry saw boxcar after boxcar flash in front of them. Red and brown paint, lettering from different rail lines, Southern Pacific, Altantic Coastline, Great Northern. The cars passed by, and finally a bright yellow caboose. The signal bell contiued a moment, then stopped, echoing in Barry's brain. He tried to focus as huge raindrops began to fall on the windshield. A flash of lightning illuminated the inside of the car and a peal of thunder shook them like an explosion. The barricade started up.

"Dad, Dad," Peter called. "Hello, Dad. We got to hurry before the game gets rained out!"

Barry jammed his foot on the brake, slammed the car in gear and tromped on the gas. The wheels spun with a a screeching sound. As soon as the barricade lifted high enough to clear the roof, Barry released the brake and the car leaped forward. His breath came in a ragged gasp as they flew over the tracks. On the other side, the road was clear, a long line of cars stopped in the opposite direction. He zoomed ahead into the empty lane, far in front of other cars. Then it dawned on him. They were alive! The train had not derailed. They were safe. Exultation filled his chest, then suddenly he realized he still had the gas all the way to the floor. The little motor screamed and the car lurched. He looked at Peter, saw fear on his face as he stared forward out the windshield.

"Dad, look out!"

Barry looked ahead just in time to see a car had crossed the double yellow line, coming straight for them. He caught a glimpse of a beat-up Cadillac, a long-nosed dog, and straight black hair around a woman's wide eyes. An expressionless face.

My God, it's Soupie!

He stuck out his arm in front of Peter, turned the wheel hard over and kept his foot on the gas. He felt the car begin to swerve as the tires clawed the road, just before a tremendous impact spun them around and around. The sensation of speed increased as he looked at the world outside. A blur of color, like a mixing bowl of a hundred different paints spun in a centrifuge. Then the air bag exploded into his face with a crashing blow. He saw white light and felt the strangest sensasion of floating.

Chapter 13

White light constellated into a galaxy of stars, silver and spinning as Barry tried to focus. Startled, he had no recollection of what was happening.

I must be drunk - he thought.

The stars slowed down to a careening halo that became the night sky. He realized that he had been spinning in a dizzy circle on his feet and sat abruptly on his bottom. His eyes wobbled in their sockets then steadied, his ears rushed to silence.

The night was still. The stars shone bright above the tops of white columns faintly luminescent in the glow of the full moon. He was sitting at the center of a small ampitheater on a marble dais. Through his robe, white linen woven in a herringbone pattern, he could feel the stone floor, cool where his buttocks made contact and cold where his naked legs extended beyond the fabric. Columns were arranged around him in a vaguely geometric pattern. Through gaps between them, he could see hills beyond, some of them with other structures, also consisting mainly of columns. In the sky, he saw the familiar tilt of Orion's Belt and the red jewel of Betelgeuse. So he seemed to be in the world, but where?

"Where am I?" He said it out loud to himself.

From behind him, there came an answer.

"You are not where or when. You are only here." The voice was deep and resonant, with a strange accent but easily understood.

He turned and saw before him a jewelled snake standing on its tail, nearly ten feet tall. It wore a white robe like a sheath, the skin that protruded being covered as if inlaid with coral and turquoise, with encrustations of bright rubies and sapphire. In the center of its head was an oval of blue lapis surrounded by gold, gleaming with a light of its own, the lapis about four inches across and six inches high, the gold border an inch all around. Its eyes were fire and onyx, like deep obsidian glass with a center of hematite.

"You are not supposed to be here." The words came from the center of the snake, emerging from its mouth only secondarily. A long, forked tongue darted in and out, black and moist. White fangs gleamed against the delicate pink background of its wide mouth.

Barry was not sure if it was the voice or the vision that mesmerized him. Or perhaps it was some potion. Before he could react, the snake bent over double and bit him squarely on the left shoulder. Terror and pain shuddered through him, the fangs like icy needles, but almost instantly the pain faded became a warm wave of comfort and well-being. He noticed he could barely feel his body at all. He sensed the benevolence of the creature and his fear evaporated.

"Go now. We may meet again."

The wondrous head turned and the snake moved aside as two women approached from the shadows. Each held a bronze taper lighted in one hand, the glow of which accentuated beautiful golden hair which flowed over their shoulders and covered their breasts. They were clothed in translucent silk veils, their bodies naked underneath. Each put out a hand, took one of his arms and helped him stand. His legs gave way immediately, but their strong fingers held him up. His toes dragged behind him on the marble as they took him down the steps of the platform and into enveloping shadow. In the dark, he saw their faces by the light of their flames, their eyes unblinking, their beautiful lips set in calm repose. A sudden breath of wind caused their wicks to flicker and go out.

After a moment of utter darkness, light spilled from an open doorway and they brought him to a room. Brocaded pillows covered the floor, rich silks flowed along the walls. His two escorts guided him in and he collapsed in a heap. The door shut silently behind him, then vanished at once among the colored silk.

Magic - he thought.

The room was lit with a series of oil lamps on pedestals, making shadows dance among the warm glow. In the middle of the room, a low table was laden with a feast of roasted chicken, the steaming aroma adding to his intoxication.

Suddenly he was starving and he set upon the chicken with his bare hands, tearing off a leg and a thigh, hot juices running down his arm and his chin as he bit in. *Succulent.* He sat on a pile of pillows next to the table and didn't stop eating until there was little but a carcass left on the ornate platter. He picked up a goblett. The honey-colored wine tasted sweet and went straight to his head. He drained the glass and set it back down, let his chin fall to his chest, gave out an enormous belch.

He fell back among the pillows with a moan, the image of his two escorts, their golden hair and gossamer veils filling his head.

Then he remembered the snake, not so much terrified as awe-struck. He looked at his shoulder, probed with his fingers. There was no sign of injury, no pain.

Here - he remembered, *the snake said there is only here.*

He closed his eyes, watched shadows dancing on his eyelids, felt his body melt into the pillows. Then he felt no sensation, no breath, only an unbroken calmness.

Here - he thought. *No where, no when. Only here. At this unbounded moment,* here *seems to extend infinitely in all directions.*

Chapter 14

A gentle light suffused his eyes and he sat up. The room was white. Deep calm filled him, as if he had been asleep for years. A low table with a porcelain basin of water was next to the couch where he lay. A lamb's wool blanket covered him, soft as down. A strange word, *flokati,* came to mind. He pushed the blanket aside, reached into the water and splashed some on his face, then drank deeply from cupped hands.

He stood and walked about the room, remembering it vaguely. It was large, about ten meters in length, and oval in shape. There were no other furnishings except the couch and the table, and at one end of the room a chamber pot which he had evidently used before, because it had urine inside. He gladly relieved himself again. At the other end of the room, he found a small pool, lined with marble and gurgling gently. Steam rose from the surface, evidently from a hot springs underneath. The water was clear and inviting. He took off his linen robe and stepped in, tentatively at first, then plunging in up to his chin. The heat was soothing and envigorating at the same time.

He closed his eyes and remembered the dream, the words of the snake. Then he remembered the words of advice from the priest. The god could appear in many forms, but often he chose the form of a snake. Barry reached involuntarily for his shoulder, where the snake had bitten him, but there was no wound and no mistaking it. He felt wonderful. Somehow he knew his time was up, but could not resist the urge to linger. The water felt so soothing, so bouyant as he floated with only his toes and his nose sticking up above the surface.

Then he remembered Peter, his only son, and his feeling of bliss turned to ice cold dread.

He dressed quickly in the robe, then walked to the other side of the room, where the door fitted flush with the curved white wall. His feet left little puddles on the marble floor, and water dripped into his eyes as he opened the portal. There was no one outside, just the clear sky, blue with a few wispy clouds, the day already beginning to feel hot. The oval room was surrounded by a larger, white ampitheater, tall columns which supported a lattice work cover that broke up the direct sun overhead. At one end was the temple proper, a series of white-walled rooms under a wooden roof in an Alpha shape.

The door to the temple was ajar and Barry could see the darkened interior. Just inside the door, there was a table and chair made of wicker wood, where one of the younger priests sat with a tablet and stylus. He looked up at Barry, then jumped to his feet, showing a wide smile.

"Good morning, Beres. How have the gods been treating you today?"

"I've had a dream."

"Good! Good! Then we're right on schedule." The younger man stood and motioned to Barry. He was dressed in a linen robe like Barry's, but there was a gold brocaded rope around his slender waist. "Would you like something to eat? Let me tell Brother Finius that you've come out of the Abaton."

"The Abaton?"

"Yes. The room with the couch and the hot springs. It's the Visitation Room where you were sleeping."

"Yes, of course. Visitation," Barry said, his tongue feeling strange. He could not recall what language they were speaking, but he had no problem understanding or making himself understood.

"Brother Finius will be pleased." The young priest left.

Barry walked around the outer wall of the temple where a row of tablets with writing on them was arranged. The letters were sharp and clear and with only a slight effort, he realized in amazement, he could read them. He examined them more closely. Black ink had been inlaid through a protective covering of wax on the wood.

. . . I confronted the dragon under the mountain, his breath like a volocano. He spoke to me kindly, advising me that my farms were to be spared, that I need only bring a monthly tribute to the cave's entrance. My daughter's life would be spared as a sign that this was true. Praise to the gods for this reasonable request . . .

. . . I fought with the snake from dawn until dusk, being bitten many times but not failing in my battle. In the end, he agreed to grant my request for healing, provided I bring an oxen and a lamb to the temple at the end of one year's continued health . . .

. . . The dog came up to us and licked my daughter's face. This was his sign to me that she would be spared great difficulty in child

*bearing and that I would be granted a grandson before the next year .
. .*

"Honorable Beres." The surprisingly familiar form of Brother
Finius waved to him from the archway. The man's bald head gleamed
white in morning sunlight.

Barry was glad to see the elderly priest. A feeling of peace
seemed to emanate from him, a feeling that got stronger as Barry
walked towards him.

"Come," Finius said. "Have some fruit. We have apricots and
figs. And oranges from Mesopotamia." He flashed white teeth and
his eyes crinkled at the corners as he smiled. The old man shuffled
across the patio.

Barry followed him onto a tiled veranda that looked to the
south. Below the edge of the balcony, the hillside fell away towards a
rugged gorge, the far side of which was about a mile away. The
sound of water greeted him, from the spring overflowing a clear pool
at one side, alongside the brightly painted outside walls of the
Visitation Room. The colorful reflection shimmered on calm water.
He seated himself across from Brother Finius at a low table
surrounded by limestone pedestals. The stone felt cool on his skin.

Before Finius could speak, a servant came with a tray of fruit
in porcelain bowls alongside a ceramic pitcher with two chalices. The
cups were ornamented with black figures on a red background. Barry
admired the vessels and selected one for himself. The servant poured
water from the pitcher, then withdrew.

"Please eat something," Finius said, motioning to the food.
"How are you feeling today?"

"I feel wonderful," Barry said. He sipped the water, which
was cool and sweet, making his spine tingle. He selected an apricot
and contemplated it before taking a bite. He chewed slowly.
"Actually, nothing seems to make sense. I have no clear memory of
coming here or who you are."

"That is not unusaul under the circumstances. This is the
Temple of Asclepius. You came here because you had a dream
inviting you to visit us. You have been troubled by dreams,
specifically of a land to the West where you believe you have a son
who is calling to you."

"Peter!"

"Yes. So the dream said. You came to us because you could find anwsers to your questions nowhere else. That was two days ago. We cleansed you seven times in the waters of the spring and then you went into the Abaton, the Visitation Chamber. I haven't seen you since. My assistant tells me you have had another dream."

"I dreamed of a great snake. But other than that I can't remember a thing."

Finius smiled knowingly. "The god Asclepius appears often in that form. Contact with him may result in a temporary loss of memory. We told you so before you entered the Visitation Room, but of course, you don't remember. Let me assure you, it will pass."

The sense of well-being Barry felt seemed to falter, like a wave rippling through a calm pond. "I don't understand."

"What you had was far more than a dream. It was a visitation. Dreams give us only what we are able to drink in, as you have a goblet of water. The visitation is an encounter with the god himself, like being plunged into the sea. In a sense, the experience drinks you."

"How do I know my memory will come back?"

"The soul is like a palimpsest," Finius explained. "As we live, impressions and images of our lives are laid down on it like writing on papyrus. Each experience is written on top of the previous one, but they are not erased, simply covered over. Our experiences remain available as memories, perhaps as dreams. Some of us are able to see them at will, or conjur them up, and they come to our aid when needed, in their own time and in their own way. Does that make sense?"

"It doesn't sound reassuring."

"Oh, but it should. If you take a tablet and write on it more than once, you won't be able to read either writing. Or if you write on the surface of a lake, you see nothing but ripples. With the soul, everything is recorded perfectly and can be recovered when needed, given the proper stimulation." Finius reached for a ripe fig. As he opened it and bit the fruit, he gazed at Barry tranquilly.

Barry felt torn. He tried to think about the image of the snake, but worried that there was something gravely wrong with him.

Finius came to his rescue. "Let's not get ahead of ourselves. First of all, tell me what you remember from last night."

"I told you, there was a great snake."

"Before that," Finius prodded.

Suddenly, Barry remembered the halo of stars. He began there, giving each detail as it appeared in his mind's eye. He continued on, through the walk with his two beautiful escorts and the feast among the pillows.

"I don't recall falling asleep, but I remember waking up."

"Strange, isn't it?"

"Excuse me?"

Finius chuckled. "Sorry. I'm remembering my first visit to the temple. It was like I had slept my whole life and suddenly I was awake for the first time. That was how I knew I was destined to become a priest."

"You came here for healing, too?"

"When I was a young man. I didn't seem to fit in with the others in the world. I'd been raised on a farm, working from dawn to dark. Then one summer I took a journey into Athens to see the way they lived. I stayed on through winter, took a job in a quarry breaking my back every day for a meager diet and a place to sleep. Anything was better than scratching in the dirt for wheat and watching sheep copulate."

"I know what you mean." Suddenly a memory of Barry's own childhood rushed through his mind. A flock of sheep in a pen, a rocky hillside rising up behind a farm house with a thatched straw roof. A feeling of revulsion and anxiety made him recoil. The memory seemed to be his, although it was distant. Finius' words made it seem all too fresh.

"There is something else I'd like you to do," Finius said standing. "My assistant will record your experience on a tablet to keep in the temple for others to share."

Startled, Barry started to get up with Finius.

"No, please don't. I'll send him to you out here. Meanwhile, you can enjoy the morning and finish your breakfast. You've earned it." He began to shuffle away.

"But Brother Finius," Barry protested. "Is that all you have to say to me?"

Finius turned and smiled again at Barry. "Don't worry. I will see you again before you go." He waved a wrinkled hand.

Barry wondered suddenly how old Finius was. He had thought not more than fifty, but suddenly he seemed much older.

About as old as I feel - he told himself, selecting a small orange from the bowl. It had been peeled carefully, and when Barry broke it open, drops of juice glistened like diamonds in the sun. The delicious scent nearly overwhelmed him.

Barry readied to leave the temple a few hours later, dressed in a woolen tunic gathered at the waist by a leather belt with a short sword. He had no other possessions, other than a pair of worn sandals and a small pouch. Brother Finius had embraced him warmly in his own chambers after he had finished dressing.

"I'm sorry you have to leave so soon, but I'm glad you received what you came for," Finius said. "It is customary to give a gift, so that your troubles do not return. I have this for you."

He held out a leather necklace with a wooden medallion on it in the shape of a snake biting its own tail. He placed it around Barry's neck.

"To remember your time with us," Finius said.

Barry had reached for the pouch at his waist, which he had noticed before to contain a dozen gold coins. He poured the coins into his palm.

"Then I will give something to you, also," he said. He held the coins out to Finius.

"No," Finius said. "You must never give more than half."

Barry took six gold coins and placed them in Finius' hand.

Finius smiled warmly. "The gods will remember you for your generosity."

They embraced again. Barry felt the old man's frail frame, but a vibrant energy came from him. He turned to go, then stopped.

"I don't know where I'm going. I barely remember who I am."

"It will pass," Finius said. "Besides," he shrugged, "there is only one path." Then, almost as an afterthought, he added, "You can always come back here if you get lost."

The path leading away from the temple was wide enough for five men to walk abreast. It wound its way down the side of the mountain, roughly following the bounding stream. At several places, Barry had to wade across shallow fords, sometimes using limestone boulders as stepping stones. He was soon in the valley below where the path was swallowed by woods. After a short time walking in the woods, he had lost all sense of direction, the sunlight jabbing through the tops of the trees in bright shafts.

The path ended at the edge of the sea. A small hut rested on a wooden dock with tiny waves lapping at its pilings. The sea was as calm as a lake and moored to the dock was a small sailboat. Barry knew at once what he had to do.

He cast off the line and turned the bow towards the open sea.

He used the oars until he had passed the headland, where a mild breeze picked up and he raised the single sail. The prow cut through the water and a slight wake followed him. He headed west.

Before very long, he lost sight of the island and was alone on the sea. Then he noticed a bank of clouds approaching. The water became rough and the wind turned opposite of where he wanted to go. In a few moments clouds covered the sky and the breeze had turned to a steady flow. The sky darkened and he sensed by the smell of the air that it was about to rain.

Undeterred, Barry stood at the bow of the tiny boat and felt the wind rushing past him. He spread his arms wide and breathed in steadily. He felt the wind begin to lift him and his feet left the boat. He hovered for a moment then rose higher and higher. Soon he was in the clouds. He knew where he had to go and the wind was lifting him higher and in the right direction, west. He forgot about the boat and set his eyes upward, trying to pierce the cloud. As he breathed in he could feel himself continuing to rise.

When he broke through the top of the cloud he was enveloped in the brilliant light of the sun. The tops of the clouds were shining white below him and it seemed as if he could see forever. But all he could think about was finding Peter.

He pressed on through the air, faster and faster, the wind singing in his ears.

Epilogue

The lake was beginning to ruffle in the middle as an evening breeze blew down the slopes and over the water, still chilled from the snow-capped summit. The splash of a strike kicked up in the smooth wake behind Peter's float and tension bent his rod double.

"I got him!"

The fish ran deep and tried to head back to the middle of the lake, but Peter brought him up short, carefully but firmly. A second later, the rainbow broke the surface in a graceful leap.

"Aw, did you see that?"

His dad met his eye, then turned back to watch the battle.

Peter scrambled for a better foothold on the granite boulder, part of a gray stone wall that made up the south shore of the lake. From there the bottom dropped off steeply into an underwater canyon, plugged at one end by a dam. Other anglers plied the water between Peter and the dam, most of them also having good luck in the calm evening. He reeled the trout into the shallows, where Dad ended its journey in the bottom of a wide net. Peter unhooked the shimmering fish the from the dry fly and held it up for his mother to see.

She stood up on the rock shore, clapping her hands together, a look of pure happiness on her face.

"You catch 'em, I'll cook 'em," she called out. It turned out she was pretty terrific at preparing trout on the Coleman camp stove, and telling stories around the campfire, too.

Peter deftly put the rainbow on the stringer with several other tasty-looking fish and readied his spinning reel to cast out again.

One more big one ought to do it for tonight - he thought.

He reached back and flung his line in a high arch across the sky. The clouds were tinted pink on one edge from the beginning of sunset, and Peter could clearly see his fly settle on top of where his float plopped down.

I'm really getting to be quite a fisherman - he told himself as he eyed the fly expectantly. Slowly he began to reel in the float, creating the little motorboat wake behind it. And *Whammo!*

He watched his son reel in another fish, pride swelling in his chest. Barry's right shoulder was still in a sling from when it had been dislocated in the car crash. He could drive a car, but he couldn't quite manage a fishing rod. Peter would have to take care of that this year. So far, so good.

The crash had put an end to their journey together and had nearly ended their lives. The driver of the other car, Sophia Sorensen had been pronounced dead at the scene. Peter had been unhurt, saved by the air bag on the passenger side, but Barry had dislocated his shoulder when his own bag inflated. Sophia's dog had survived the impact without a scratch, but was disconsolate over his master's body. The paramedics had to struggle to keep him away while they tried unsuccessfully to save the broken woman. Finally, Peter had stepped in to take the dog aside, comforting him as best he could, then took him along in the ambulance to the hospital with Dad.

After the memorial service, it had been Peter's idea what to do with Soupie's ashes. The idea to bring the dog along had been a joint effort, less a concession than an affirmation by Barry that something important had happened to all of them.

They scattered Soupie's ashes at sunset the first night of their trip. It had taken some explaining to Mom what they were up to, but she had gone along in the end. The ashes floated in a slow circle, eddying towards the spill way before being sucked down and through. By now, they were spread all up and down the length of Bishop Creek.

Peter had his own tent this year at the campsite, which suited him just fine. He could change his clothes without anybody watching and the muffled sounds his parents made in their tent didn't keep him awake at all. In fact, he was sleeping like a baby.

Tonight, he had shared his trout with the multi-colored mut with the long snout that had attached himself to Peter when his master was killed. A lot of things had fallen into place after that ill-fated trip to Wrigley Field, not the least of which was deciding to call the dog *Soupie*.

The End

Acknowledgements

No book is written in a vacuum, although the writer must face many trials and struggles alone. We have the help of those who have gone before us and those who surround us to encourage us. I wish to acknowledge Reverend John A. Sanford for his wisdom as presented in his book <u>Healing and Wholeness</u>, written in 1977, but very close to me today. His mother, Agnes Sanford, was a friend and prayer partner of my mother back in the '50's and I was fortunate enough to attend lectures by Jack at a local church in San Diego.

I also wish to thank the members of Ken Kuhlken's writers' group for their encouragement and suggestions on how to improve my work.

Finally, I wish to thank my wife, Karen, for her patience in putting up with me all these years, when so much of the time I was busy writing and not available to her. I also want to appreciate her wonderful garden, which is truly an Eden for me with "rivers flowing underneath", and one of my greatest inspirations.

www.ingramcontent.com/pod-product-compliance
Lightning Source LLC
Chambersburg PA
CBHW020633130626
46552CB00003B/1212